William Shakespeare's Henry V: A Retelling in Prose

David Bruce

Published by David Bruce, 2022.

This is a work of fiction. Similarities to real people, places, or events are entirely coincidental.

WILLIAM SHAKESPEARE'S HENRY V: A RETELLING IN PROSE

First edition. July 24, 2022.

Copyright © 2022 David Bruce.

ISBN: 979-8201562106

Written by David Bruce.

Table of Contents

Dedication

Dedicated to Carl Eugene Bruce and Josephine Saturday Bruce

My father, Carl Eugene Bruce, died on 24 October 2013. He used to work for Ohio Power, and at one time, his job was to shut off the electricity of people who had not paid their bills. He sometimes would find a home with an impoverished mother and some children. Instead of shutting off their electricity, he would tell the mother that she needed to pay her bill or soon her electricity would be shut off. He would write on a form that no one was home when he stopped by because if no one was home he did not have to shut off their electricity.

The best good deed that anyone ever did for my father occurred after a storm that knocked down many power lines. He and other linemen worked long hours and got wet and cold. Their feet were freezing because water got into their boots and soaked their socks. Fortunately, a kind woman gave my father and the other linemen dry socks to wear.

My mother, Josephine Saturday Bruce, died on 14 June 2003. She used to work at a store that sold clothing. One day, an impoverished mother with a baby clothed in rags walked into the store and started shoplifting in an interesting way: The mother took the rags off her baby and dressed the infant in new clothing. My mother knew that this mother could not afford to buy the clothing, but she helped the mother dress her baby and then she watched as the mother walked out of the store without paying.

***

The doing of good deeds is important. As a free person, you can choose to live your life as a good person or as a bad person. To be a good person, do good deeds. To be a bad person, do bad deeds. If you do good deeds, you will become good. If you do bad deeds, you will become bad. To become the person you want to be, act as if you already are that kind of person. Each of us chooses what kind of person we will become. To become a good person, do the things a good person does. To become a bad person, do the things a bad person does. The opportunity to take action to become the kind of person you want to be is yours.

Human beings have free will. According to the Babylonian Niddah 16b, whenever a baby is to be conceived, the Lailah (angel in charge of contraception) takes the drop of semen that will result in the conception and asks God, "Sovereign of the Universe, what is going to be the fate of this drop? Will it develop into a robust or into a weak person? An intelligent or a stupid person? A wealthy or a poor person?" The Lailah asks all these questions, but it does not ask, "Will it develop into a righteous or a wicked person?" The answer to that question lies in the decisions to be freely made by the human being that is the result of the conception.

A Buddhist monk visiting a class wrote this on the chalkboard: "EVERYONE WANTS TO SAVE THE WORLD, BUT NO ONE WANTS TO HELP MOM DO THE DISHES." The students laughed, but the monk then said, "Statistically, it's highly unlikely that any of you will ever have the opportunity to run into a burning orphanage and rescue an infant. But, in the smallest gesture of kindness — a warm smile, holding the door for the person behind you, shoveling the driveway of the elderly person next door — you have committed an act of immeasurable profundity, because to each of us, our life is our universe."

In her book titled *I Have Chosen to Stay and Fight*, comedian Margaret Cho writes, "I believe that we get complimentary snack-size portions of the afterlife, and we all receive them in a different way." For Ms. Cho, many of her snack-size portions of the afterlife come in hip hop music. Other people get different snack-size portions of the afterlife, and we all must be on the lookout for them when they come our way. And perhaps doing good deeds and experiencing good deeds are snack-size portions of the afterlife.

The Zen master Gisan was taking a bath. The water was too hot, so he asked a student to add some cold water to the bath. The student brought a bucket of cold water, added some cold water to the bath, and then threw the rest of the water on a rocky path. Gisan scolded the student: "Everything can be used. Why did you waste the rest of the water by pouring it on the path? There are some plants nearby which could have used the water. What right do you have to waste even a drop of water?" The student became enlightened and changed his name to Tekisui, which means "Drop of Water."

Cover Illustration for *William Shakespeare's Henry V: A Retelling in Prose*:

Henry V of England — Illustration from Cassell's *History of England* — Century Edition — published circa 1902

Educate yourself.

Read like a wolf eats.

Feel free to give this book to anyone free of charge.

Be excellent to each other.

In this retelling, as in all my retellings, I have tried to make the work of literature accessible to modern readers who may lack some of the knowledge about mythology, religion, and history that the literary work's contemporary audience had.

Do you know a language other than English? If you do, I give you permission to translate this book, copyright your translation, publish or self-publish it, and keep all the royalties for yourself. (Do give me credit, of course, for the original retelling.)

I would like to see my retellings of classic literature used in schools, so I give permission to the country of Finland (and all other countries) to give copies of this book to all students forever. I also give permission to the state of Texas (and all other states) to give copies of this book to all students forever. I also give permission to all teachers to give copies of this book to all students forever.

Teachers need not actually teach my retellings. Teachers are welcome to give students copies of my eBooks as background material. For example, if they are teaching Homer's *Iliad* and *Odyssey*, teachers are welcome to give students copies of my *Virgil's* Aeneid: A Retelling in Prose and tell students, "Here's another ancient epic you may want to read in your spare time."

CAST OF CHARACTERS

On the Side of the English

KING HENRY THE FIFTH (1387-1422)

DUKE OF GLOUCESTER, Brother to the King

DUKE OF BEDFORD, Brother to the King

DUKE OF EXETER, Uncle to the King

DUKE OF YORK, Cousin to the King

EARL OF SALISBURY

EARL OF WESTMORELAND, Cousin by marriage to the King, and Brother-in-Law to the Duke of Exeter

EARL OF WARWICK

ARCHBISHOP OF CANTERBURY

BISHOP OF ELY

RICHARD, EARL OF CAMBRIDGE, conspirator against King Henry V

HENRY, LORD SCROOP OF MASHAM, conspirator against King Henry V

SIR THOMAS GREY OF NORTHUMBERLAND, conspirator against King Henry V

SIR THOMAS ERPINGHAM, loyal to King Henry V

GOWER, an English Captain

FLUELLEN, a Welsh Captain

MACMORRIS, an Irish Captain

JAMY, a Scottish Captain

JOHN BATES, Soldier in King Henry V's army

ALEXANDER COURT, Soldier in King Henry V's army

MICHAEL WILLIAMS, Soldier in King Henry V's army

PISTOL, NYM, BARDOLPH, Soldiers in King Henry V's army, and former friends of Prince Hal

Boy

A Herald

On the Side of the French

CHARLES THE SIXTH, King of France

ISABEL, Queen of France

LEWIS, the Dauphin

KATHERINE, Daughter to Charles and Isabel

ALICE, Lady attending on the Princess Katherine

DUKES OF BURGUNDY, ORLEANS, and BOURBON

The CONSTABLE OF FRANCE, the chief military officer of France

RAMBURES and GRANDPRÉ, French Lords

MONTJOY, a French Herald

Governor of Harfleur

Ambassadors to the King of England

Other Characters

Hostess of the Boar's Head Tavern, formerly Mistress Nell Quickly, and now married to Pistol

Chorus, consisting of one male

Lords, Ladies, Officers, French and English Soldiers, Citizens, Messengers, and Attendants

Nota Bene

Scene: England and France

Time: 1414-1420

Religion: Catholic. The Protestant Reformation does not start until 1517, when Martin Luther's "95 Theses" become public. In 1534 the Church of England separated from the Roman Catholic Church because of a dispute over the annulment of the marriage of King Henry VIII to Catherine of Aragon. Pope Clement VII excommunicated King Henry VIII.

It is a good idea to remember this quotation by L.P. Hartley: "The past is a foreign country: they do things differently there."

See "Appendix A: Brief Historical Background" if you need a very brief refresher on English history.

PROLOGUE

Imagine that the year is 1599, and a single male character takes the stage in a round theater in England. This character is known as the Chorus, and he will introduce the play the way a single male character known as the Prologue would, and he will also appear at the beginnings of Acts 2-5 to comment on the action of the play and the way that he hopes the audience will react to it; he will also appear as the Epilogue at the end of the play.

The Chorus strides onto the stage and says, "I wish that I could be inspired by a Muse of fire. Of the four elements — fire, water, air, and earth — that people of my time think make up all that exists, fire is the element that rises highest. Anyone who wishes to tell the story that is told in this play must be mightily inspired and capable of the best poetic creation.

"I also wish that this small stage were an entire Kingdom, and I wish that the actors were Princes, and the members of the audience were Kings who would watch this majestic scene!

"If my wishes would become reality, then the warlike Harry — King Henry V of England — would be like himself. He would be like the real Harry as Harry really existed and he would take on himself the bearing of Mars, the Roman god of war. At Harry's heels would appear famine, swords, and fire — the instruments of war — that would be tied to a single leash held in Harry's hand. These three instruments of war would crouch like hounds waiting for Harry's command to go into action.

"But forgive us, all you gentlemen and gentlewomen. We on stage here are not spirits of the great and mighty dead who have been raised out of their graves. We have not been raised from the graves; we are dull and uninspired actors — and a playwright — who have dared to portray great men and great events on this platform that is called a stage. Can this small stage hold the vast battlefields of France? Can we cram within this wooden O — this round theater made out of wood — the actual helmets that frightened the air at Agincourt, where in 1415 King Henry V defeated the French although he and his soldiers were vastly outnumbered?

"Please pardon us for our presumption! A zero is a curved figure of arithmetic. A zero is naught, but if you add it to the weakest position of a number — the far right — it can turn the number 100,000 into the number 1,000,000! We actors are also naught, but while we are on stage acting as great people doing great acts, let us affect your imaginations so that you visualize the scene as it ought to be seen.

"Imagine that within the surroundings of the walls of this theater are now confined two mighty Monarchies — the English and the French Kingdom — who challenge each other. They have high, soaring, and close-to-each-other fronts that the perilous narrow ocean — the English Channel — keeps apart. The English cliffs of Dover and the French cliffs of Calais challenge each other.

"Use your imaginations to improve on and mend our imperfections. Thousands of soldiers fought in the war; a few actors will 'fight' on this stage. Use your imagination to take one 'fighting' actor and turn that single actor into a thousand fighting soldiers who fight a huge and dangerous battle in front of you.

"When we actors talk about horses, imagine that you see them stamping on the soil and leaving their hoofprints behind them.

"We need your imaginations to properly equip our Kings, to move them from country to country and battlefield to battlefield, and place to place, and to jump over years so that the events of 1414-1420 can take place on this stage in only a couple of hours that can easily be measured by a two-hour hourglass.

"I, the Chorus, will help you to leap over the years — I will, occasionally, let you know when years have passed.

"But now, let me, like a Prologue, ask you humbly for your humble patience. Please listen to this play with gentle courtesy, for hearing and seeing are both important, and please judge this play with kindness."

CHAPTER 1

— 1.1 —

In an antechamber in King Henry V's palace — the Palace of Westminster in London — the Archbishop of Canterbury said to the Bishop of Ely, "My lord, I'll tell you something important: that same bill is now being proposed that in 1410 — the eleventh year of the reign of our last King, Henry IV, was likely to have been passed, and indeed it would have been passed except that the violent and unruly times turned people's attention to other, more urgent matters."

"But how, my lord, shall we resist it now?" the Bishop of Ely asked.

"We must think about how to resist this bill," the Archbishop of Canterbury replied. "If it passes against our wishes, we — the Church — lose more than half of our possessions. This bill, if passed into law, would strip away all the temporal and secular lands that devout men in their wills have given to the Church. These lands are valuable. The people who would strip these lands away from us believe that the lands' value would pay for, to the King's honor, fifteen Earls and fifteen hundred Knights, and also six thousand and two hundred good esquires; in addition, their value would maintain a hundred well-supplied almshouses to support lazars — the word comes from Lazarus the beggar and refers to chronically ill people who cannot work — and weak old people who cannot work with their bodies. Also, these lands' value would add a thousand pounds annually to the treasury of the King. All of that wealth would be taken from the Church, which is exempt from paying taxes on its lands and wealth."

"If our lands and wealth were a cup filled with wine, this bill would drink deep," the Bishop of Ely said.

"This bill would drink all the wine from the cup," the Archbishop of Canterbury exaggerated.

"How can we prevent this bill from passing and becoming law?"

"The King is full of grace and fair regard," the Archbishop of Canterbury said. "He has Christian goodness, and he is respected."

"He is a true lover of the Holy Church."

"He is a good man, but his behavior when he was youthful was undisciplined and reckless and showed no promise of future excellence," the

5

Archbishop of Canterbury said. "At that time, he was commonly known by common men as Prince Hal. However, when the breath left the body of his father, King Henry IV, immediately Prince Hal's wildness, subdued by him, seemed to die and leave his body. As soon as Prince Hal's father the King died, spiritual contemplation and careful thought and awareness of his position came to the Prince. This spiritual contemplation, like an angel, came to the Prince and whipped the offending Adam out of him. Adam committed the first sin, and sin now departed from Prince Hal's body. With sin gone, his body was like a paradise, one that could envelop and contain celestial spirits. It was like an angel took possession of the body of the person who then became King Henry V.

"Never has such a scholar so suddenly been made; Prince Hal immediately changed from a dissolute youth to a sober and serious King — one with a knowledge of theology. Never has reformation come in such a flood; the rush of flowing water scrubbed away Prince Hal's faults. The thoroughness of the cleaning process was like that of Hercules cleaning the Augean stables. King Augeas had over a thousand cattle, and his stables had not been cleaned for over 30 years. Hercules cleaned the stables in a single day by diverting the course of a river so that it flowed through the stables and washed away the manure.

"Prince Hal had been filled with willfulness and with unworthy desires that he repeatedly satisfied. Never so quickly has Hydra-headed willfulness departed as it departed from the body of this King Henry V. The Hydra was a nine-headed serpent-like sea monster. Each time one head was cut off, two more heads sprung up in its place. Hercules was able to kill the Hydra with the help of his nephew Iolaus, who used a fire-torch to cauterize the stump left behind each time a head was cut off. Unworthy desires are like the heads of the Hydra. Each time a person gives in to one unworthy desire, two more unworthy desires spring up. King Henry V was able to kill each unworthy desire the way that Hercules killed the heads of the Hydra."

Each time Heracles cut off one of the Hydra's mortal heads, his nephew Iolaus cauterized it with a torch, thus preventing more heads from growing. Heracles then cut off the immortal head and placed it under a boulder. The blood of the Hydra was poisonous, and before leaving, Heracles dipped the heads of his arrows into the Hydra's blood.

"We are blessed in the change," the Bishop of Ely said.

"Listen to King Henry V discuss matters of divinity, and you will admire his thoughts," the Archbishop of Canterbury said. "You will even have an inward wish that the King would be made a prelate — a bishop or holder of some other high ecclesiastical office. Listen to him discuss the affairs of state, and you would say that he has long been making a deep study of government. Listen to him discuss warfare, and you shall hear a discourse that is so well spoken that it is like music. Ask him about any judicial argument involving politics, and he will know the pros and the cons and the intricacies. Even if the argument is like the Gordian knot — a knot so intricate that people thought that it was impossible to untie — King Henry V will untie that knot as easily as he unties the knot of his garter that keeps his stocking up. Alexander the Great 'untied' the Gordian knot by cutting it in two with his sword, but King Henry V is the superior of Alexander the Great. When King Henry V unties the Gordian knot of a political controversy, the air, which is free to go wherever it pleases, is still. The ears of men are filled with quiet wonder as they closely listen to his sweet and honeyed sentences.

"Practical life experience is more important than theory — he could not speak so wisely about these matters unless he applied such wisdom to his own life. We must wonder where King Henry V acquired such wisdom. After all, he filled his youth with inclinations toward foolish behavior. As a youth, he enjoyed companions who were uneducated and ignorant, without manners, and frivolous. He filled his hours with riotous revels, banquets, and entertainments. No one ever saw him engage in study, retire from company, and enjoy privacy so that he could reflect upon important matters. No, Prince Hal was always in public and in crowds of the common people."

"Perhaps he is like the fruit of strawberry plants," the Bishop of Ely said. "Our culture believes that most plants are affected by the plants of other species that grow near them. Therefore, we do not allow onions and garlic to grow near most fruit bushes. However, such plants as onions and garlic do not negatively affect strawberry bushes. Strawberry bushes grow underneath the nettle, and their wholesome strawberries thrive and ripen best when the bushes' neighbors are vegetables of baser quality. Like the strawberry bushes, Prince Hal hid the seriousness of his thoughts; he kept them secret. In his case, the veil was one of wildness. But like summer grass, which grows fastest by night, Prince Hal's seriousness and wisdom, although unseen by others, yet grew because it is their nature to grow."

The Archbishop of Canterbury said, "What you say must be correct because otherwise we would have to say that the change of Prince Hal's character to the character of King Henry V is the result of a miracle, and the only true miracles are those that are recorded in the Bible. Therefore, we have to find a natural cause for the change in his character and how he has been brought to perfection."

"My good lord, what can we do now to stop or mitigate the effects of the bill that has been put forward to the House of Commons? We do not want to have more than half of the Church's wealth seized by the government. Does his majesty favor this bill, or not?"

"He seems impartial," the Archbishop of Canterbury said. "Or, rather, I should say that he leans more toward us than toward the people who support this bill. He leans more toward us because I have made an offer to his majesty, following my meeting with other clergy. This offer relates to important matters concerning France that are of concern now. To his grace the King, I have offered to give a greater sum than ever at one time the clergy has given to any of his predecessors."

"What does King Henry V think about this offer?"

"He regards it favorably," the Archbishop of Canterbury said. "However, there was not time enough then for him to hear, as I perceived his grace would have liked to have heard, the particular facts and the indisputable arguments that prove that he has true claims to particular Dukedoms in France and indeed to the crown and throne of France. Henry V, King of England, ought to also be the King of France; Henry V is directly descended from his great-grandfather, King Edward III of England, and this gives him a claim to be King of France. The mother of Edward III is the daughter of King Philip IV of France, and so Henry V of England is directly descended from King Philip III through the female line."

"What happened to interrupt your conversation with King Henry V?" the Bishop of Ely asked.

"The French ambassador arrived and asked for an audience with the King to be scheduled. The hour, I think, has come for us to go and listen to the King. Is it four o'clock?"

"Yes, it is."

"Then let us go into the King's presence so that we can hear the French ambassador's message. I can guess the content of that message even before the Frenchman speaks a word of it."

"I will go with you," the Bishop of Ely said. "I long to hear the French ambassador's message."

— 1.2 —

At the Palace of Westminster in London, several people entered the King's Presence Chamber, the large room in which King Henry V received official visitors. Those people were King Henry V himself, the Duke of Gloucester, the Duke of Bedford, the Duke of Exeter, the Earl of Warwick, the Earl of Westmoreland, and several attendants.

King Henry V asked, "Where is my gracious Lord of Canterbury?"

Exeter replied, "He is not here in the Presence Chamber."

"Send for him, good uncle," King Henry V said.

"Shall we call in the ambassador, my liege?" Westmoreland asked.

"Not yet, my cousin," King Henry V replied. He then used the royal plural when he said, "Before we hear him, we want to have some doubts resolved about some matters of importance that burden our thoughts, concerning us and France."

The Archbishop of Canterbury and the Bishop of Ely entered the King's Presence Chamber.

The Archbishop of Canterbury said to the King, "May God and his angels guard your sacred throne and may you long grace it with your presence!"

"Surely, we thank you," King Henry V replied. "My learned lord, please proceed and justly and religiously explain why the Salic Law — the law that bars women from inheriting the throne — that they have in France either should, or should not, bar us in our claim to the throne of France.

"And God forbid, my dear Lord of good Christian faith, that you should deliberately misinterpret, wrest, or distort your reading, or lay a burden on your soul — a soul that understands the difference between good and evil — by using sophistry to raise illegitimate claims to the throne. Such illegitimate claims clash with the truth. I wish to know whether my claim to the French throne is legitimate or illegitimate because God knows how many men who are now healthy shall drop their blood in support of what your reverence shall

9

incite us to do. If my claim is illegitimate and you make me believe that i[t] is legitimate, many men shall die for an unjust cause. Should my claim b[e] legitimate, many of our men shall still die, but they will die for a just cause.

"Therefore, take heed how you influence our person and how you awake[n] our sleeping sword of war. We command you, in the name of God, to tak[e] heed because never did two such Kingdoms contend in war against each othe[r] without much fall of blood, whose guiltless drops are every one a woe and a sor[e] complaint against him whose wrongdoing gives edge unto the swords that tak[e] short human lives and make them shorter. If men die, they should not die fo[r] an unjust cause. Their lives should not be wasted.

"Under this solemn appeal, speak, my lord. We will hear and note what yo[u] say and believe in our heart that what you speak is in your conscience as pure a[s] sin after it has been washed with baptism. We will believe that what you say i[s] the truth whether you say that our claim is legitimate or illegitimate."

The Archbishop of Canterbury did not mention Isabella, the daughter o[f] King Philip IV of France, but it was on her that King Henry V's claim to th[e] French throne rested.

King Philip III of France fathered King Philip IV of France, who fathere[d] Isabella, who lived the longest of King Philip IV's four children. If female[s] could inherit the throne, she would have inherited it.

Isabella married King Edward II of England, and they became the parent[s] of King Edward III of England.

King Edward III of England fathered John of Gaunt, who was the Duke o[f] Lancaster.

John of Gaunt fathered Henry Bolingbroke, who became King Henry IV of England.

King Henry IV of England fathered King Henry V of England, who now wondered whether his claim to the French throne was legitimate or illegitimate[.] He was directly descended from King Philip III of France, but through th[e] *female* line.

The then-present King of France, Charles VI, could claim direct descen[t] from King Philip III of France through the *male* line.

King Philip III of France fathered King Philip VI of France, who fathere[d] King John II of France.

King John II of France fathered King Charles V of France, who fathered the then-present King of France, Charles VI.

Of course, many people were Kings of France in between King Philip III of France (reigned 1270-1285) and the then-present King of France, Charles VI, whose reign began in 1380:

King Philip III of France reigned 1270-1285. He was also known as Philip III the Bold.

King Philip IV of France reigned 1285-1314. He was also known as Philip the Fair.

King Louis X of France reigned 1314-1316. He was also known as Louis the Quarreler.

King John I of France reigned in 1316. He was alive for only five days and is also known as John the Posthumous.

King Philip V of France reigned 1316-1322. He was also known as Philip the Tall.

King Charles IV of France reigned 1322-1328. He was also known as Charles the Fair.

King Philip VI of France reigned 1328-1350. He was also known as Philip VI the Fortunate.

King John II of France reigned 1350-1364. He was also known as John the Good.

King Charles V of France reigned 1364-1380. He was also known as Charles V the Wise.

The reign of Charles VI of France began in 1380. He was also known as Charles VI the Mad.

The year in which King Henry V of England was inquiring into the legitimacy of his claim to the throne of France was 1414. His claim would be legitimate if the throne could be inherited through the female line; after all, a later age saw England ruled by Queen Elizabeth I. However, his claim would be illegitimate if the throne could NOT be inherited through the female line.

The Bishop of Canterbury said, "Listen to me, gracious sovereign, and you peers, who owe yourselves, your lives, and your services to this imperial throne. I say 'imperial' because you, Henry V, ought to be the King of more than one country. There is no bar against your highness' claim to France except for this, which the French produce from Pharamond, King of the Salian Franks, a Germanic people: '*In terram Salicam mulieres ne succedant.*' This is Latin for 'No woman shall succeed in the Salic land.' In other words, no woman shall inherit the throne in the Salic land.' The French incorrectly and unjustly interpret 'Salic land' to be the realm of France, and they regard King Pharamond as the founder of this law and female bar to the throne. Yet their own French authors affirm that the Salic land is in Germany, between the Sala and the Elbe rivers, where Charlemagne, aka Charles the Great, having subdued the Saxons, left behind and settled certain Frenchmen, who, holding in disdain the German women because of the women's unchaste conduct, established then this law: To wit, no female should inherit the throne in the Salic land.

"As I said before, the Salic land lies in between the Sala and the Elbe rivers. Today in Germany the land is called Meissen. Therefore, it is certain that the Salic law was not devised for and does not apply to the realm of France.

"In addition, the French did not possess the Salic land until 379 years after the death of King Pharamond, who was falsely supposed to be the founder of this law. King Pharamond died in 426 A.D., and Charlemagne subdued the Saxons and colonized the Salic land with Frenchmen in the year 805 A.D.

"I will now refer to a number of French Kings:

"King Chlothar I, King of the Franks, who reigned 511-561.

"King Childeric III, King of the Franks, who reigned 743-751 or 743-752.

"King Pepin, King of the Franks, who reigned 751-768 or 752-768. He was also known as Pepin the Short and as Pepin the Younger.

"King Charlemagne, aka Charles the Great, who reigned 768-814.

"King Louis I, who reigned 814-840. He was also known as Louis the Pious.

"King Charles II, aka Charles the Bald, who reigned 840-877. He also called himself 'the Great,' which has led people to confuse him with Charlemagne. He was King of the Franks (840-877), King of Western Francia (840-877), and the Holy Roman Emperor (875-877).

"King Hugh Capet, King of the Franks, who reigned 987-996.

"King Louis IX, who reigned 1226-1270. He is also known as Saint Louis IX.

"The French writers state that King Pepin, who deposed King Childeric III, was heir general, which means that he inherited the throne — whether through the male or the female line did not matter. As heir general, he made claim and title to the crown of France because he was descended from Blithild, who was the daughter of King Chlothar I. As you can see, the French have used the female line to help determine who shall be King.

"In addition, let us consider Hugh Capet, who usurped the crown that should have belonged to Charles the Duke of Lorraine, who was sole male heir of the true line and stock of Charles the Great, aka Charlemagne. Hugh Capet, to improve his claim to the title of King with some shows of truth, although, to be honest, his claim to the title of King was corrupt and worthless, pretended to be heir to the Lady Lingare, who was the daughter of King Charles II, aka Charles the Bald, who was the son of Louis the Pious. Louis the Pious was also known as King Louis I, King of the Franks, and as Holy Roman Emperor Louis I. Louis the Pious was the son of Charlemagne, with whom he was co-Emperor of the Holy Roman Empire. As you can see, the French have used the female line to help determine who shall be King.

"In addition, let us consider King Louis IX, who was the sole heir to the usurper Hugh Capet. King Louis IX felt guilty wearing the crown of France until he was satisfied that beautiful Queen Isabel, his grandmother, was directly descended from the Lady Ermengare, who was the daughter of Charles the Duke of Lorraine. By the marriage of Isabel to his grandfather, King Philip II, the line of Charles the Great, aka Charlemagne, was reunited to the crown of France. As you can see, the French have used the female line to help determine who shall be King.

"This information may be hard to follow, but if you follow it, it will be as clear as the summer Sun that King Pepin's title, and King Hugh Capet's claim, and King Lewis IX's satisfaction, all appear to hold in right and title of the female line. All of them have used the female line to justify their being on the throne of France, and the same is true of other French Kings until this present day. Nevertheless, they use the Salic law to prevent your highness from claiming the throne of France from the female line. Instead, they choose to try to hide their own actions in a net through whose holes they can easily be seen. They choose to try to hide their own actions rather than openly acknowledge that their titles are crooked and stolen from you and your ancestors."

King Henry V asked, "May I with justice and a clear conscience make this claim to the throne of France?"

"Yes, dread sovereign," the Archbishop of Canterbury said. "Should there be any sin, let it fall on my head! I can say that because I know that your claim is not sinful. For in the book of Numbers is written that when the man dies with no male heirs, let the inheritance descend unto the daughter. To be specific, Numbers 27:8 states, 'And thou shalt speak unto the children of Israel, saying, If a man die, and have no son, then ye shall cause his inheritance to pass unto his daughter.' Gracious lord, stand up for your own rights; unfurl your flag although it means going to war and shedding blood, and remember your mighty ancestors.

"Go, my dread lord, to the tomb of your great-grandfather, King Edward III, from whom arises your claim to the throne of France. Invoke his warlike spirit, and invoke the warlike spirit of your great-uncle, Edward the Black Prince, the son of Edward III. He was called the Black Prince because of his black armor. In 1346, on a French battlefield, he played the role of a hero as he and his soldiers defeated the entire French army in the Battle of Crécy. His most mighty father — a lion, a Monarch — on a hill stood smiling as he beheld his lion's whelp glut himself on the blood of French nobility. We English were noble on that day! We fought the entire French army with only half of the English army and defeated it. The other half of our army was on the hill with King Edward III. Our soldiers there stood laughing as they watched the battle. They had no work to do and were cold because they needed not exert themselves!"

King Henry V thought, *Actually, two-thirds of the English army were fighting. Only one-third of the English army was on the hill with my great-grandfather. The patriotism of the Archbishop of Canterbury has understandably led him to exaggerate.*

The Bishop of Ely said, "Remember all these valiant dead and with your powerful arm renew their feats. You are their heir; you sit upon their throne; the blood and courage that made them renowned runs in your veins; and you, my thrice-powerful liege, are in the May morning of your youth — you are ripe for exploits and mighty enterprises. You are triply powerful because you are the heir of these warriors, you sit upon the throne of England, and you have the courage of your warrior ancestors."

Exeter said, "Your brother Kings and Monarchs of the earth all expect that you will rouse yourself and seek what is rightfully yours, as did the former lions of your blood."

Westmoreland said, "They know that your grace has a just cause, enough wealth, and enough military strength, as in fact your highness has. Never has any King of England had richer nobles and more loyal subjects, whose hearts have left their bodies here in England and instead are metaphorically inside military tents on the battlefields of France."

The Archbishop of Canterbury said, "Let their bodies follow their hearts, my dear liege, to win the throne of France, which is rightfully yours, with bloodshed and sword and fire. To aid you in pursuing your claim to the throne of France we of the Church will raise for your highness such a mighty sum as never have the clergy at one time given to any of your ancestors."

King Henry V said, "We must not only arm to invade France, but we must also calculate the number of troops needed to defend England against the Scots, who will attack our country when they believe it is advantageous for them to do so."

The Archbishop of Canterbury said, "Those people who live in the Marches — the land bordering Scotland — will serve as a wall that is sufficient to defend the rest of our country from the pilfering borderers. The lords of the Marches have armed men."

"I am not referring only to the fast-galloping Scottish raiders," King Henry V said. "I fear the armed invasion of the Scots as a whole. They have always been dangerous and unreliable neighbors to us. You can read in histories that Edward III, my great-grandfather, never went with his armed forces into France without the Scots pouring into his defenseless England like the tide waters pour onto a beach. The Scots would attack with great forces at their full strength the English land whose soldiers had been gleaned from its fields, and they would surround and lay a grievous siege on castles and towns. England was defenseless because so many of its soldiers were fighting in France, and so the English citizens left behind in England shook and trembled because Scotland is such a bad neighbor."

"England has been more frightened than it has been harmed, my liege," the Archbishop of Canterbury objected. "Look at English history. When all of England's chivalrous nobles were in France, and England was like a widow mourning the loss of the nobles, England not only has well defended itself but also captured and imprisoned the King of Scotland as if he were a stray beast. In 1346, while Edward III was in France, King David II of Scotland was captured and it was thought that he was taken to France and given to Edward III so that his fame could be swelled by making prisoners of the Kings of foreign lands. In addition, the capture of King David II of Scotland has helped to make England's history as rich with praise as is the oozy bottom of the sea rich with sunken wrecked ships and with immeasurable wealth."

Westmoreland, who was Warden of the northern Marches, knew much about the military threat of Scotland. He said to the King, "Remember this very old and true saying, 'If you want to win France, / Then with Scotland first begin.' Once the eagle warriors of England leave to seek prey, to England's unguarded nest the weasel Scot comes sneaking and so breaks into and sucks the protein out of her Princely eggshells. The Scot plays the mouse when England the cat is absent, acting in accordance with the proverb 'While the cat's away, the mice will play.' Like mice, the Scots will break into and ruin more food than they can eat."

"It follows then the cat must stay at home," Exeter said, "but yet that is distorted logic — that particular conclusion does not necessarily follow. After all, we have locks to safeguard necessaries, and we have ingenious traps to catch the petty thieves. While the armed hand fights abroad, the cautious and prudent head defends itself at home. Government and society are like music. Government has high and low and lower positions and social classes, and music has high and low and lower notes and harmonies. If the parts of government and society work together properly, and the parts of the music work together properly, the result is harmonious and agreeable. If all of the citizens remaining in England work together while Henry V is in France with his army, England shall be safe."

"That is why Heaven has divided the body politic of Humankind into different positions performing different functions," the Archbishop of Canterbury said. "Human effort is continual, and it has as its target obedience to the will of God and the will of their King.

"Look at how the honeybees work. They have an instinctive government that can teach us, the citizens of a human Kingdom, orderly action. Honeybees have a King — actually, a Queen — bee. Honeybees also have various kinds of officers. Some bees are like magistrates who administer justice at home. Other bees are like merchants who venture to trade abroad. Other bees are like soldiers, and their stings are their weapons. They plunder the summer's velvet buds, and they merrily march with their plunder home to the royal tent of their Emperor, who busily surveys the singing masons as they build roofs of gold, the civil citizens molding the cells of the honeycombs, the poor working bees crowding in with their heavy burdens at his narrow gate, the serious-eyed justice with his surly hum or hmm as he hands over to threatening executors the lazy yawning drone.

"I infer from all of this that many people, all of whom work toward one target, may work at various jobs to achieve a single goal.

"They are like many arrows, shot by many archers standing in different places, that fly toward one target.

"They are like many roads around one town that go toward and meet in that town.

"They are like many fresh-water streams that flow toward and run into the same salt sea.

"They are like the lines of a Sun-dial that all run toward and meet in the center of the Sun-dial.

"So may a thousand actions done by different groups of people, once begun, end by achieving one goal with great success and without defeat.

"Therefore, go to France, my liege. Divide your happy English soldiers into four armies. Take one army with you to France, and with them you shall make all France shake. If we, with three such armies left at home, cannot defend our own doors from the dog of war, let us be torn to pieces and let our nation lose its reputation for hardiness and statesmanship."

King Henry V said, "Call in the messengers sent from the Dauphin, who is the son of the King of France and the supposed heir to the throne."

A few attendants exited the Presence Chamber.

King Henry V said, "Now the doubts we had concerning our claim to the throne of France have been resolved, and I have decided to pursue our claim. By God's help, and yours, you nobles who are the noble sinews of our power, France being ours because of our legitimate claim to the throne, we will bend France so that it respects the authority of England, or if it will not bend, we will break it all to pieces. Either we will sit on the throne of France and rule with complete sovereignty both it and all her almost Kingly Dukedoms, or these bones of mine will lie in an unworthy grave, without a monument, with no memorial inscription over them. Either our history — the biography of King Henry V — shall with full mouth speak freely of our acts in acquiring the throne of France and ruling as King of France, or else our grave will be like a Turkish slave whose tongue has been cut out to stop the spreading of state secrets. Unless we become King of France, our grave shall have a tongueless mouth and lack accomplishments to boast about. Unless we become King of France, our grave shall not even be honored with an epitaph made of perishable wax."

The French ambassadors entered the King's Presence Chamber.

King Henry V said, "Now we are well prepared to know what our fair kinsman the Dauphin has to say to us, for we hear that this greeting is from him, not from the King of France."

In fact, King Henry V and the Dauphin were kinsmen; they were distantly related.

The first ambassador asked, "Will your majesty give us permission to state clearly the message we bring to you from the Dauphin, or shall we use diplomatic language to indirectly and tactfully state what the Dauphin wants us to tell you?"

"We are no tyrant; instead, we are a Christian King," King Henry V replied. "I keep even my strongest emotions under control; they are under control as much as are the wretched inmates of our prisons. Therefore with frank and uncurbed plain language, tell us the Dauphin's message to us."

The first ambassador said, "Briefly and with few words, I say this: Your highness recently sent ambassadors to France to claim some certain Dukedoms, which you believe are yours because of your great predecessor King Edward III. In answer to your claim, the Dauphin our master says that you have not yet grown out of your youth, that you are still the immature youth that you were, and he tells you that there is nothing in France that can be won by performing the fast and nimble dance that is known as the galliard. You cannot revel yourself into any French Dukedoms. The Dauphin therefore sends you something that he thinks is more suitable for you, this container of treasure. He insists that you accept the treasure and give up your claim to the French Dukedoms. This is the message that the Dauphin required us to bring to you."

King Henry V said to Exeter, "What is the treasure, uncle?"

"A container of tennis balls, my liege."

The tennis balls were made of leather and stuffed with horsehair. The game of royal tennis was played on a paved oblong court that was surrounded by walls. Between the two longer walls, a rope or low net was stretched. The two shorter walls had holes that were called hazards; a ball hit into a hazard scored a point. A point was also scored when a ball bounced twice before the opposing player could hit it. The opposing player would chase after the ball to hit it with a stringed racket.

King Henry V said to the French ambassadors, "We are glad the Dauphin is so pleasant with us, and we thank you for his present and your pains.

"When we have marched our rackets to these balls, we will, in France, by God's grace, play a set that shall strike the Dauphin's father's crown into the hazard. Tell the Dauphin he has made a match with such a wrangler that all the courts of France will be disturbed with chases.

"We intend to march our army to the place from where these tennis balls came: France. There, the game that we will play is called war. We intend to play so well that we will strike the Dauphin's father's crown from off his head and onto ours. Tell the Dauphin he has made a match with such a warrior that all the noble courts will be disturbed by English soldiers chasing fleeing French nobles.

"We admit that we well understand the Dauphin's reference to our younger, wilder days. He does not understand how useful they were to us. When we were young, we never valued this poor seat — the throne — of England; therefore, living away from the court, we gave ourself to barbarous license and behaved riotously, as is common: Men are merriest when they are away from home.

"But tell the Dauphin that I will keep my throne and I will act like a King and show my sail of greatness — my military banners and coat of arms — when I rise up out of my throne in France.

"So that in the future I could appear to be more glorious, in my youth I set aside my majesty and plodded like a working man, but I will rise from my throne in France with so full a glory that I will dazzle all the eyes in France. I will strike the Dauphin blind when he attempts to look at me.

"Tell the pleasant Prince — the Dauphin — this joke of his has turned his tennis balls into cannonballs. His soul shall be charged with the wasteful vengeance that shall fly with the cannonballs — his joke will create many thousands of widows. He will fail to cheat me out of my French throne, but he will succeed in cheating many French wives out of their dear husbands and he will succeed in cheating many French mothers out of their sons. He will be responsible for the deaths of thousands and for the tearing down of French castles. Some are not yet begotten and not yet born who shall have cause to curse the Dauphin's scorn.

"But all this lies within the will of God, to Whom I do appeal, and in Whose name you shall tell the Dauphin I am coming to get revenge — I will put forth my effort in a righteous cause that is approved by God. So leave from here in peace and tell the Dauphin that his jest will be shown to be of only shallow wit when thousands more weep at it than ever laughed at it."

Henry V said to some attendants, "Escort these French ambassadors away from here. Give them safe conduct."

He said to the French ambassadors, "Fare you well."

Some English attendants and all the French ambassadors exited.

Exeter said, "This was a merry message."

Henry V replied, "We hope to make the sender blush at it. We want to make the Dauphin ashamed of it, and we want his cheeks and face to be red with blood."

He added, "Therefore, my lords, take every opportunity to advance our expedition against France. For we have now no thought in us but thoughts about France, save those thoughts we have about God — our thoughts about God are more important than any other business.

"Therefore, let our army for these wars be soon collected and gathered together and all things thought upon that may with reasonable swiftness add more feathers to our wings. We wish to start this action in France quickly.

"With God to guide us, we will chide this childish Dauphin at his father's door.

"Therefore, let every man now employ his thoughts in setting our noble enterprise into action."

CHAPTER 2

Prologue

The Chorus walked on stage and said, "Now all the youth of England are on fire to go to war in France, and the silken clothing needed to court the ladies is laid away in the wardrobe to be replaced by metal armor. Now thrive the armorers, and only thoughts of gaining honor reign in the breast of every man: they sell land now to buy a horse to ride to war. They wish to follow Henry V, the exemplar of all Christian Kings, into battle. They are as eager to quickly follow the King as they would be if they were as fast as Mercury, the messenger of the gods — a messenger whose winged heels and winged helmet flew him quickly through the air.

"Now the expectation of winning glory in war is everywhere, and men think of a sword that is hidden from the hilt to the point with the crowns of Emperors who rule more than one country, the crowns of Kings who rule a single country, and the coronets worn by nobles. These emblems of rule have been promised to Harry and his followers.

"The French, advised by good intelligence of this most serious preparation for dreadful war that causes them to shake with fear, attempt to foil the English invasion with a treacherous plot.

"Oh, England! You are a small country, but you have greatness within you. You are like a great heart enclosed in a small body. What great things you would accomplish, what honor you would earn, if all your citizens were kind and obeyed natural law and respected your King!

"But see your fault! France has found in you a nest of hollow bosoms. Three Englishmen lack patriotism and loyalty to their King, and France fills the pockets of these three treacherous men with coins.

"These three corrupted men — Richard, Earl of Cambridge; Henry, Lord Scroop of Masham; and Sir Thomas Grey, Knight, of Northumberland — accepted the gilt of France and so bear the guilt of treason. They have formed a conspiracy with France, which fears the English King and army, and have agreed to kill this model of Kingship: King Henry V.

"If Hell and treason keep their promises, they will kill Henry V in Southampton before he sets sail for France.

"Be patient, audience, and we will help you to cope with the great distance that must be traveled on our stage.

"Now the traitors have received the bribe that France promised them, now the King is traveling from London to Southampton, and soon he will set sail to France.

"Audience, sit in your seats in the theater, and we will safely convey you soon to France, and safely bring you back, too. We will charm the English Channel so that you can gently travel both ways. If we are able to, we will not make even one audience member seasick or disgusted with our play.

"But before we join the King in Southampton, let us enjoy a scene set in London."

— 2.1 —

On a street in London, Corporal Nym and Lieutenant Bardolph were speaking together. Soon to join them was Pistol, who was an Ensign, aka sub-Lieutenant. Bardolph was the highest ranking of the three, and Nym was the lowest ranking. All three were low-lifes living in Eastside. Nym's name came from "nim," which means "a thief" or "to steal." Pistol's name was pronounced "pizzle," which also meant "penis." The Chorus had said that every Englishman is thinking about gaining honor on the battlefield, but Nym, Bardolph, and Pistol were exceptions. The Chorus had also said that the men of England are as eager to quickly follow the King as they would be if they were as fast as winged Mercury, but perhaps we ought to remember that Mercury is, among other things, the god of thieves.

"Good to see you, Corporal Nym," Bardolph said.

"Good morning, Lieutenant Bardolph," Nym replied.

"Are Ensign Pistol and you friends yet?" Bardolph asked.

"For my part, I do not care whether we are friends," Nym said. "I do not care whether we are friends. I say little, but when the time comes for me to smile I will smile, perhaps to pretend that I am friends with him or perhaps because I have gotten my revenge on him, but that shall be as it may. I dare not fight, but I will bluster. I will close my eyes and hold out my iron sword. It is a simple sword, but so what? I can use it to toast cheese on its point, and I can draw it and let it grow cold while another man's sword does the same, and there's an end to another man and an end to my discourse."

Nym liked to think that he said little, spoke mysteriously, and kept his thoughts to himself. Much of what he said and thought made little sense.

Bardolph replied, "I will buy you two breakfast if that will make you friends again. Let all of us be three sworn brothers as we go to France. Be friendly again with Pistol, good Corporal Nym."

"Truly, I will live as long as I may, that's certainly the truth, and when I cannot live any longer, I will do as I may; that is my final bid, and that is the last resort of it."

"It is certain, Corporal, that Pistol is married to Nell Quickly," Bardolph said, "and certainly she did you wrong. She was legally bound to marry you."

"I cannot tell where the truth lies," Nym said. "Things must be as they may: Men must sleep, and they must have their throats about them at that time, and some people say that knives have sharp edges. It must be as it may: Though patience be a tired mare, yet she will plod — patience will reach success in the end. There must be conclusions. Well, I cannot tell."

Pistol and Nell Quickly, the hostess of the Boar's Head Inn in Eastcheap, walked up to Bardolph and Nym.

Bardolph said, "Here comes Ensign Pistol and his wife. Good Corporal Nym, control yourself here. We are on a public street."

Nym said, "How are you, host Pistol!"

Pistol, who liked to use extravagant language, was outraged. He was a superior officer to Nym, who should have referred to him by his military title: Ensign. Of course, by marrying Nell Quickly, the hostess of an inn, Pistol had become the host of that inn.

Pistol said, "Base mongrel, are you calling me your host? Now, by my hand, I swear that I scorn the term. I also swear that my Nell shall not keep lodgers in her inn."

Nell Quickly said, "Truly, I shall keep no lodgers. It is impossible for us to give room and board to a dozen or fourteen gentlewomen who live honestly by the prick of their needles. Why? Because everyone will think that they make their living by a different sort of prick, and everyone will think that we are keeping a bawdy house."

Thinking that it was time for him to bluster, Nym drew his sword. Pistol did the same.

Nell Quickly said, "Heavens! Look! He has drawn his sword! We shall see willful adultery and murder committed."

As usual, Nell Quickly had mixed up her words. Adultery is always willfully committed; she had probably meant to say that murder would be willfully committed. And why bring up adultery? Did she believe that Pistol would be the murder victim and she would go back to Nym?

Bardolph said, "Good Lieutenant! Good Corporal! Do not fight in a public street!"

Bardolph was a Lieutenant. Nym was a Corporal. Pistol was an Ancient, aka Ensign.

Nym said scornfully to Pistol, "Pish!"

Pistol scornfully replied, "Pish for you, Iceland dog! You are a shaggy-haired dog and a prick-eared cur of Iceland!"

Nell Quickly said, "Good Corporal Nym, show your valor, and put up your sword."

She had spoken more wisely than she knew. Usually, to show one's valor, a man would draw his sword and fight, but Nym had no valor, so to show his (lack of) valor, he should sheathe his sword.

Both Nym and Pistol sheathed their swords, but they would soon draw them again. No matter. The only way either of them would die in this fight would be for one of them to trip and accidentally fall on his own sword.

The shaggy-haired Nym said to Pistol, "Will you amscray and shove off with me to a place where we can fight without interruption? I would have you *solus*."

Not knowing that *solus* is Latin for "alone," Pistol thought that he had been insulted: "*Solus*, outrageous dog? Oh, vile viper! I will shove that *solus* in your most marvelous face. I will shove that *solus* in your teeth, and in your throat, and in your hateful lungs, and yes, in your stomach, by God, and, which is worse, within your nasty mouth! I will shove that *solus* all the way to your bowels. For I can take fire and grow angry, and Pistol's cock is up, and flashing fire will follow."

Later, people would listen to accounts of the "fight," and they would laugh when they heard "Pistol's cock is up." But Pistol meant that metaphorically his gun, aka pistol, was cocked and ready to fire.

"You sound as if you were a conjuror performing an incantation for an exorcism," Nym said, "but it won't work on me. I am not the son of Barba, a fiend who fought fiercely after assuming the shape of a lion. I have the humor — am in the mood — to beat you rather well. Once fired, pistols are foul and dirty, and they need to be cleaned and scoured with a ramrod. If you use foul language against me, Pistol, I will scour you with my rapier, to put it as decently as I can. If you would walk with me to a place out of sight of the public, I would prick your guts a little, to put it as decently as I can, and that's how I feel about it."

"You are a vile braggart and a damned furious creature!" Pistol shouted. "Your grave gapes, and doting death is near and desirous of taking you, and therefore prepare to exhale your final breath."

Some of Pistol's extravagant language came from the action-filled, bombastic plays he enjoyed watching and listening to.

Bardolph drew his sword and said to Nym and Pistol, "Hear me, listen to what I say: He who strikes the first stroke, I'll run him through with my sword up to the hilt, I swear on my profession as a soldier."

Pistol replied, "This is an oath of mickle — much — might; and so my fury shall abate."

He sheathed his sword, then Nym sheathed his sword, and finally Bardolph sheathed his sword.

Pistol said to Nym, "Give me your fist; give me your fore-paw. I have to admit that your spirit is very brave."

Nym replied, "I will cut your throat at one time or another, to put it as decently as I can, and that's how I feel about it."

Pistol replied in bad French and a lack of knowledge about how many words make up a word, "'*Couple a gorge*!' That is the word."

He had meant to say, "*Coupez la gorge*," which means "Cut his throat."

He added, "I defy you, Nym, again. Oh, hairy hound of Crete, did you think that you could get my spouse? That is not going to happen. No, instead, make your way to the hospital and find yourself a woman. Look in the powdering tub of infamy — the heated tub in which ill people sit in order to sweat out venereal disease, and find Doll Tearsheet — who is just like Cressida, a loose woman who suffers from the pox — and promise to marry her. I have …."

Pistol stopped and thought and then said, "I have, and I will hold, the *quondam* Quickly. Once she was Miss Quickly and now she is Mrs. Pistol, and she is the only woman for me — *pauca*, there's enough. Go to."

Pistol knew a few words of Latin, although people who really knew Latin knew that Pistol knew fewer Latin words than he thought he did. *Quondam* meant "former," and "Quickly" was his wife's maiden name. *Pauca* was short for *pauca verba* and meant "few words."

A boy — Sir John Falstaff's page, aka young servant — arrived and said, "My host Pistol, you must come to my master, Falstaff, and you, hostess, must come, too. Falstaff is very sick, and he wants to go to bed."

The boy looked at Bardolph, whose face was fiery-red from his alcoholism, and joked, "Good Bardolph, put your fiery-red face between his sheets so that you can warm them up like a warming-pan."

He added, "Truly, Falstaff is very ill."

"Go away, you rogue!" Bardolph, who could be sensitive about his face, yelled at the boy.

Nell Quickly said about the precocious boy, "Indeed, one of these days he will be hung and his hanging carcass will provide a feast for crows."

She then said about Falstaff, "The King has killed his heart."

She was referring to when Prince Hal had been crowned as King Henry V. Falstaff had not treated him like a King, calling him by the familiar name "Hal." Falstaff should have bowed before his sovereign. Instead, he had challenged Henry V to reject him. If Henry V had not rejected him, Falstaff would have looted the treasury. Fortunately for England, King Henry V had rejected Falstaff and never again saw him. Nell Quickly thought that Falstaff's heart had broken because the King had rejected him, but Falstaff's heart had broken because he could not loot the treasury. He had hoped to run wild in England when Prince Hal was crowned King Henry V.

Nell Quickly said to Pistol, "Good husband, go home as soon as you can."

Nell Quickly and the boy left to go to Sir John Falstaff.

Bardolph said to Nym and Pistol, "Come, shall I make you two friends? We must go to France together, so why the Devil should we keep knives to cut one another's throats?"

Pistol said, "Let our friendship last until the rivers overflow their banks and flood the land and until the Devils in Hell howl in fury because they do not have enough evil souls to torment!"

Nym was willing to be friends again — provided a proviso was met: "You'll pay me the eight shillings I won from you at betting?"

Pistol, who was uneager to fulfill this request, replied, "Base is the slave who pays."

Nym said, "That money I must have now, and that's the long and the short of it."

Pistol said, "Let courage decide. Let's fight over that money."

Both Pistol and Nym drew their swords.

Bardolph drew his sword and said, "By this sword, I will kill the first man who makes the first thrust. I swear by this sword that I will kill him."

Pistol said, "He swore by his sword, and that is an oath, and a soldier's oath is an oath that must be kept."

Pistol sheathed his sword.

Bardolph said, "Corporal Nym, if you will be friends with Pistol, then be friends, but if you will not be friends with Pistol, why, then, be enemies with me, too. Please, sheathe your sword."

Nym asked Pistol, "Shall I have the eight shillings I won from you at betting?"

Pistol said, "Yes," and Nym sheathed his sword, and then Bardolph sheathed his sword.

Pistol said to Nym, "I shall give you a noble, a coin that is worth a little less than eight shillings. I will pay you the rest with liquor. That way, we will be friends, and brothers, too. I'll live by Nym, and Nym shall live by me. Is not this just? I can make back the money I pay to you. I will be a sutler to the camp of soldiers — I will supply the soldiers with provisions — and that will give me ample opportunity to make some profits, some of them by honest means — profits will accrue. Give me your hand and let's shake on it."

Nym asked again, "I shall have my noble?"

Pistol replied, "Yes — in cash most justly and honestly paid."

Nym replied, "Well, then, that's the long and the short of it."

Nell Quickly returned and said to them, "If you were born of woman, come quickly and see Sir John. Poor man! He is so shaken from a burning quotidian tertian fever. He has one fever that visits him every day, and another fever that visits him every other day. He is in a piteous predicament, and seeing him will rouse your pity. Sweet men, go and see him.”

Nym said, “The King has caused Sir John’s melancholy — that’s the plain truth of it.”

Pistol said, “Nym, you have spoken the truth; Sir John’s heart has been fracted and corroborated — broken and confirmed to be broken.”

Nym replied, “The King is a good King, but we must say it because it is true — he has some strange moods and does some strange things. As King, he can indulge his thoughts and do whatever he wishes.”

Pistol said, “Let us go and condole Sir John Falstaff. The Knight will die, but we, lambkins, will continue to live.”

— 2.2 —

In a council chamber in Southampton, the Duke of Exeter, the Duke of Bedford, and the Earl of Westmoreland were discussing three traitors whose treason had not yet been openly revealed. King Henry V and the English army were in Southampton because they would sail from there to France. The three lords were there because they expected to receive commissions to rule England in the King’s absence.

Bedford said, “I swear to God that his grace is rash to trust these three traitors.”

Exeter replied, “The traitors will be arrested soon.”

“How confidently they bear themselves!” Westmoreland said. “They are good actors. They act as if they were completely dutiful and faithful and loyal to the King.”

Bedford said, “The King has complete knowledge of their treason and of all that they intend to do. The traitors do not at all know that their plans have been revealed to the King.”

“The worst traitor is Henry, Lord Scroop of Masham, the man with whom the King was most friendly,” Exeter said. “In our society, friends of the same sex sometimes sleep in the same bed. Nothing sexual occurs, and no one thinks anything negative about it. A man who once shared the King’s bed is now a traitor, although the King has surfeited his appetite with gracious favors. I cannot imagine why Scroop would sell his King’s life for money. Scroop has formed a plan to treacherously kill the King.”

Trumpets sounded, and King Henry V and his attendants, and the three traitors — Richard, Earl of Cambridge; Henry, Lord Scroop of Masham; and Sir Thomas Grey, Knight, of Northumberland — entered the council chamber.

King Henry V said, "The wind is fair, and we will soon board our ship."

He then said to the three traitors, "My Lord of Cambridge, and my kind Lord of Masham, and you, my noble Knight, tell me your thoughts. Do you think that the army we have brought with us will be able to cut their passage through the army of France? Will they be able to execute the work that I have planned for them and for which I have assembled them?"

Scroop replied, "No doubt, my liege, they can if each man does his best."

"I don't doubt that each man will do his best," King Henry V said. "We are absolutely convinced that each man who goes with us from here to France is in perfect agreement with us, and we are absolutely convinced that we will not leave behind any man who does not wish us success and conquest."

"Never has there been a Monarch more feared and loved than is your majesty," Cambridge said. "I doubt that you have a single subject who has a heavy and uneasy heart; all of your subjects sit in the sweet shade of your government."

Grey said, "That is true. Once, your father had enemies, but those enemies are now your friends. They steeped their bitter gall in sweet honey and now they serve you with hearts that are dutiful and zealous to obey you."

"We therefore have great cause to be thankful," Henry V said. "We would prefer not to be able to use our hand than to neglect to reward people of desert and merit in accordance with their weight and worthiness."

"Your people are all the more eager to serve you and work energetically with sinews of steel because of their hope to be rewarded for their incessant service," Scroop said.

"We think that you are correct," Henry V replied.

The King then said, "Uncle Exeter, set free the man who was arrested yesterday because he railed against our person. We are taking into consideration that he was drunk and that the excess of wine made him rail against us. Now that he has sobered up and is regretting what he did, we pardon him."

Scroop said, "You are being merciful but rash in pardoning him. Let him be punished, sovereign, lest his bad example breed — because it has not been punished — more of the same kind."

Henry V replied, "Although that is a possibility, I am inclined to be merciful."

Cambridge said, "Your highness can be merciful and yet punish him, too."

Grey said, "Your highness, you will be merciful if you allow him to live after he has been severely punished."

King Henry V said, "You three care about me so much that you strongly encourage me to punish this poor wretch! But if we cannot close our eyes so we do not notice little faults that occur because of the distemper of alcohol, how will be we be able to open our eyes wide enough to show our astonishment when serious crimes, capital crimes punishable by death and that have been chewed, swallowed, and digested — with malice aforethought — appear before us?

"We will still set free that man, although Cambridge, Scroop, and Grey, because they dearly care about the tender preservation of our person, would have him punished.

"But now let us turn to our business in France: Who are the recently appointed regents who will govern England in our absence?"

"I am one of them, my lord," Cambridge said. "Your highness told me to ask for my written commission today."

"You told me the same thing, my liege," Scroop said.

"As you did me, my royal sovereign," Grey said.

"Then, Richard, Earl of Cambridge, there is your written commission," Henry V said, handing him one of the three scrolls he was carrying. "There is yours, Lord Scroop of Masham; and, Sir Knight, Grey, of Northumberland, this one is yours. Read them, and realize that I know your true worth."

He added, "My Lord of Westmoreland, and Uncle Exeter, we will board the ships tonight."

The three traitors looked at their papers and turned pale with fear. The papers informed them that the King knew about their treason and their plot to murder him.

Henry V said to them, "Why, how are you now, gentlemen! What words do you see in those papers that make you lose so much color in your faces? Look, everyone, how their faces have changed! Their cheeks are white like paper. Why, what words did you read there that have turned you into cowards and chased your blood away from your cheeks? Red blood is the sign of courage, and you have no red blood in your cheeks."

Cambridge knelt and said, "I do confess my fault, I am guilty, and I beg your highness for mercy."

Grey and Scroop both knelt and said, "We also appeal to your highness for mercy."

King Henry V said, "The mercy that was alive in us just now has been suppressed and killed because of the advice that you gave to me. You must not dare, for shame, to talk of mercy because your own words turn against you, as dogs can turn upon their masters, and bite you.

"Look, my loyal Princes, and my loyal noble peers, at these English monsters!

"Look at my Lord of Cambridge here. All of you know how our respect for him made us want to give him all things appropriate to his honor. Yet Cambridge has, for a few crowns of light weight, for treacherous money, lightly and readily conspired and sworn to join the plot of France to kill us here in Southampton.

"This Knight also swore the same thing that Cambridge did although he was also indebted to me, the King, for the good things I have given to him.

"What shall I say to you, Lord Scroop? You cruelly ungrateful, savage, and inhuman creature! You knew all my secrets, you knew the deepest part of my soul, you almost might have used me as your own minter and maker of money. How is it possible that a foreign bribe could extract from you even enough evil to harm one of my fingers? This is so strange and unexpected that even though the truth of it appears as clearly as black and white, my eye will scarcely see it. My eyes scarcely believe what is clearly visible in front of them!

"Treason and murder have ever kept company together; they are like two Devils yoked together and sworn to help each other achieve the other's goals. The two Devils openly work together in what for them is a natural cause. That is expected, and it causes no astonishment.

"But you, against all natural order, brought in astonishment to accompany treason and murder. No one could have expected you to conspire to take my life. You have no good reason to do so.

"Whatever cunning fiend — whatever Devil — it was that worked upon you and got you to act so perversely has been applauded in Hell for its excellence. All other Devils that suggest and tempt men to commit treason do so by unskillfully patching up and cobbling together reasons and veneers and ideas that seem to be ethical and pious but really are not. These Devils tempt people to do damnable things by convincing them that they are doing the right thing. But the Devil that persuaded you to do damnable actions simply told you to stand up and rebel without giving you a reason why you ought to commit treason."

King Henry V looked at Scroop, who was kneeling before him the way that a man would kneel before the King who would Knight him — dubbing a person Knight means giving that person the title of Knight — by touching his shoulder with a sword and saying, "I dub thee Knight. Arise, Sir —"

He then said, "The only reason a Devil could have given you for why you should commit treason is so that you could be dubbed 'Traitor.'"

King Henry V remembered 1 Peter 5:8: "*Be sober, be vigilant; because your adversary the Devil, as a roaring lion, walketh about, seeking whom he may devour*" and he said, "If that same demon that has gulled you in this way should with his lion gait walk throughout the whole world, he might return to vast Hell and tell the legions of angels, 'I can never win a soul as easily as I won the soul of that Englishman.'

"You Scroop, have infected the sweetness of trust with suspicion. You make it hard for me to trust anyone ever again. What evidence can I now seek to determine whether men are good? Do men seem to be dutiful? Why, so did you. Do men seem to be grave and learned? Why, so did you. Do men come from a noble family? Why, so did you. Do men seem to be religious? Why, so did you. Are men moderate in their diet? Are men free from excessive emotions, whether of mirth or anger? Are men constant in spirit, not excessively changing their minds? Are they furnished with and display good personal characteristics and courtesy? Do they not only look but also listen, and use their best judgment to evaluate evidence and arrive at the truth? You seemed to be such a man, a man whose evil had been purged out of him, and thus your fall has left a kind of blot — now, even a man whose excellent character is fully loaded with the best virtues is regarded by me with some suspicion.

"I will weep for you because this revolt of yours, I think, is like another fall of man: the fall of Adam, who ate the fruit of the Tree of Knowledge of Good and Evil."

He said to Exeter, "The faults of these three traitors are manifest and open and revealed. Arrest them in accordance with the law, and God forgive them for their evil deeds!"

Exeter said to the three traitors, "I arrest you for high treason, Richard, Earl of Cambridge. I arrest you for high treason, Henry, Lord Scroop of Masham. I arrest you for high treason, Thomas Grey, Knight, of Northumberland."

Scroop said, "Our evil plot God justly has uncovered, and I regret my sin more than I regret my death. I beg your highness to forgive my sin, although my body will pay the price of it."

Cambridge said, "As for me, the gold of France did not seduce me, although I admit it was a motive to do sooner the treason that I had already intended to commit. But I thank God that I have been prevented from carrying out my plan. I will rejoice at this prevention even as I endure my punishment, and I beg God and you to pardon me."

Grey said, "Never has a faithful subject rejoiced more at the discovery and prevention of most dangerous treason than I rejoice at this hour even though it is my own dangerous treason that has been revealed. I have been stopped from carrying out a damned plot. Pardon my sin — but not my body — sovereign."

King Henry V said, "May God in His mercy forgive you! Now hear your sentence. You have conspired against our royal person. You have joined forces with a known enemy to our country and have received golden money to murder me. In doing this, you would have sold and sentenced your King to slaughter, you would have sold and sentenced his Princes and his peers to servitude, you would have sold and sentenced his subjects to oppression and contempt, and you would have sold and sentenced his whole Kingdom to desolation. As far as our own life is concerned, we seek no revenge, but we must so cherish our Kingdom's safety — safety that you have sought to ruin — that we deliver you to her laws. Therefore, poor miserable wretches, go to your death. May God give you the fortitude to endure your death and give you true repentance for all your serious offences!"

He ordered the guards, "Take them away."

The three traitors got to their feet, and the guards led them to the place of
execution.

King Henry V then said, "Now, lords, let us turn our attention to France.
This enterprise in France shall be as glorious to you as it is to us. We do not
doubt that this war shall be successful and with good fortune to us since God
so graciously has brought to light this dangerous treason that was lurking in
our way to kill us and stop the war before it started. We doubt not now but
that every obstacle has been removed that stood in our way. So let us go forth,
dear countrymen. Let us deliver our army into the hand of God, and let us get
started immediately. Let's go cheerfully to sea and see the signs of war advance.
I will not be King of England unless I can also be King of France."

— 2.3 —

In front of a tavern in London, Pistol, Nell Quickly, Nym, Bardolph, and
the boy who had been Sir John Falstaff's page were standing and talking about
the death of Sir John, which had occurred just after midnight.

Nell Quickly said to Pistol, "Please, honey-sweet husband, let me
accompany you to Staines, a town on the way to Southampton."

"No, because my manly heart yearns — it is grieving," Pistol replied.

He said to the others, "Bardolph, be blithe. Nym, rouse your vaunting veins.
Boy, bristle your courage up. Falstaff is dead, and therefore we must yearn — we
must grieve."

Anyone overhearing Pistol might laugh. The verb "yearn" means to want
someone. To want someone means either to grieve for someone or to feel sexual
desire for someone. Some other words could be understood in more than one
way. Someone overhearing Pistol could think that he was saying this:

"My manly heart feels sexual desire. Bardolph, do something to make
yourself very, very happy. Nym, rouse your vaunting veins — the ones that are
in the appendage that hangs below your waist. Boy, make your 'courage' — the
appendage that hangs below your waist — bristle and rise up. Falstaff is dead,
but we live, and therefore we must feel sexual desire."

Bardolph said, "I wish that I were with Falstaff, wherever he is, whether in
Heaven or in Hell!"

Nell Quickly said, "I am sure that he's not in Hell; instead, he's in Arthur's
bosom, if ever man went to Arthur's bosom."

Nell Quickly meant Abraham's bosom rather than the bosom of King Arthur, famous in part for his Knights of the round table.

She added, "Falstaff made a finer end than the one that would have sent him to Hell. He died as if he had been a christom child — a child who died sinless and baptized in its first month of life. He died just between twelve and one — as the old belief states, his life ebbed with the tide. After I saw him fumble with the sheets and play with the flowers lying on the bed and smile because his fingers were not obeying his commands, I knew that he was dying because of these signs and other signs: His nose was as sharp as a pen, and he babbled about green fields. I tried to comfort him and to give him good advice: 'How are you, Sir John?' I asked, and said, 'Be cheerful!' He cried out 'God, God, God!' three or four times. Now I, to comfort him, advised him that he should not think of God; I said that I hoped there was no need to trouble himself with any such thoughts yet. So he told me to lay more clothes on his feet because they were cold. I put my hand under the sheets and felt his feet, and they were as cold as any stone; then I felt up to his knees, and they were as cold as any stone, and so upward and upward, and all the parts of his body were as cold as any stone."

Nell Quickly was being unintentionally bawdy as she spoke. One meaning of "stone" is "testicle," so we have an image of Nell Quickly moving her hands from Falstaff's feet higher and higher on his body until she felt his testicles.

Falstaff's death was similar to the death of Socrates as recounted in Plato's *Phaedo*. Socrates drank hemlock, as required by the jurors of Athens when he was found guilty at his trial. As the poison worked, Socrates' body grew colder and colder, starting with his feet and working upward.

Falstaff's reference to "green fields" may have been a reference to this famous Biblical passage (Psalm 23, King James Version):

The Lord is my shepherd; I shall not want. He maketh me to lie down in green pastures: he leadeth me beside the still waters. He restoreth my soul: he leadeth me in the paths of righteousness for his name's sake. Yea, though I walk through the valley of the shadow of death, I will fear no evil: for thou art with me; thy rod and thy staff they comfort me. Thou preparest a table before me in the presence of mine enemies: thou anointest my head with oil; my cup runneth over. Surely goodness and mercy shall follow me all the days of my life: and I will dwell in the house of the Lord for ever.

Nym said, "They say he cried out against alcohol."

Nell Quickly said, "Yes, he did."

Bardolph added, "And he cried out against women."

Nell Quickly said, "No, he did not."

The boy said, "Yes, he did. He said that women were Devils incarnate."

The word "incarnate" reminded Nell Quickly of another word: "He could never abide carnation; it was a color he never liked."

The earlier Falstaff who had not been actively dying was not a fan of the incarnation of God: Jesus.

The boy said, "Falstaff said once that the Devil would have his soul because he pursued women."

Nell Quickly said, "Falstaff did, occasionally, touch on the topic of women."

The boy thought, *He also occasionally touched women.*

Nell Quickly continued, "But when he talked about women, he was rheumatic, and talked of the whore of Babylon."

The boy thought, *Falstaff was not rheumatic; Nell probably means lunatic. On his deathbed, Falstaff was in and out of his right mind. This is something that sometimes happens to alcoholics when they die. Falstaff's nose grew "sharp as a pen," as Nell Quickly said. The faces of the dying sometimes grow thinner and their noses seem to grow sharper.*

The boy asked, "Do you remember when he saw a flea light upon Bardolph's nose, and he said that it was a black soul burning in Hell-fire?"

Bardolph said, "Well, the fuel is gone that maintained that fire. The consumption of alcohol is what made my nose red, and Falstaff bought that alcohol for me. That is the way that he paid me for my services to him."

The dying Falstaff was not like the living Falstaff. The living Falstaff enjoyed sack, and he enjoyed women. His testicles were hot, not cold. He enjoyed laughing and making people laugh. When he prayed, he prayed as a joke. He was in his right mind, although that mind was evil.

At the end of Falstaff's life, he was trying to pray or to recite a Biblical Psalm. He was afraid of being damned to Hell. He was also repenting his sins of drunkenness and fornication.

As evil as Falstaff's life had been, he may have died well. According to Christian theology, an evil man who sincerely repents on his deathbed will be accepted into Paradise.

Nym asked, "Shall we amscray and shove off? The King will soon sail from Southampton."

Pistol said, "Come, let's leave."

He said to his wife, Nell Quickly, "My love, give me your lips. Kiss me. Look after my property and prevent it from being stolen. Keep on the alert; remember these words of wisdom: 'Cash down, no credit.' Trust no one; oaths are like straws, and men's promises are like thin wafer-cakes. Promises and pie crusts are easily broken. Promises are good, but deeds are better. A dog named 'Brag' is good, but a dog named 'Steadfast' is better, my love. Therefore, let *Caveto* be your counselor."

The Latin *caveto* means, "Be careful" or "Beware." *Caveto* is the second/third-person singular future active imperative of *caveō*.

Pistol added, "Go, clear your crystals — wipe the tears from your eyes. Yoke-fellows in arms, let us go to France. We will be like leeches that attach themselves to horses, my boys, and suck and suck and suck the blood of the French!"

The boy said, "Blood is an unhealthy food, they say."

Pistol said, "Touch my wife's soft mouth — kiss her — and let's march."

Bardolph said, "Farewell, hostess," and kissed Nell Quickly.

Nym said, "I cannot kiss her, that is the long and short of it; but I say, *adieu*."

Pistol said to his wife, "I command you to practice good household management and stay out of trouble."

His wife replied, "Farewell; *adieu*."

The males left.

— 2.4 —

In the French King's palace, several men were meeting: the French King, the Dauphin, the Dukes of Berri and Bretagne, the Constable, and others. The Constable of France was the commander-in-chief of the army in the absence of the King.

The King of France said, "Now comes the English King and his army upon us with England's full power, and we must be extra careful to put up a first-class defense. Therefore, the Dukes of Berri and of Bretagne, of Brabant and of Orleans, shall go forth, and you, too, Prince Dauphin, as swiftly as you can, to strengthen and reinforce our fortifications with men of courage and with defensive equipment. The King of England's hostile approach is as fierce as a whirlpool that violently sucks in waters. We ought, therefore, to be as provident in making preparations for the future as fear has taught us to be as a result of recent battles in which the English soldiers whom we had fatally neglected left many French dead upon our battlefields. We ought to remember the English victories in the Battle of Crécy in 1346 and in the Battle of Poitiers in 1356."

The Dauphin said, "My most redoubted — formidable and respected — father, it is certainly fitting that we arm ourselves against the foe. Peace should not dull a Kingdom and make it lazy; even when no war has been declared and no reason for war is known to exist, defenses should be maintained, armies should be assembled, and other preparations should be made as if a war were expected. Therefore, I say that it is fitting we all go forth to view the sick and feeble parts of France. Let us do so with no show of fear; let us show no more fear than if we had heard that the English were busying themselves with a traditional Whitsun Morris dance. After all, my good liege, England is badly Kinged; the scepter of England is so fantastically borne by a vain, giddy, shallow, capricious youth that no one needs to fear England."

The Constable said, "That is not the case, Prince Dauphin! You are too much mistaken about King Henry V. Talk to and question the ambassadors that you sent to his court. They will tell you about the great dignity with which he heard your message to him, how well supplied with noble counselors, how modest in raising objections, and how altogether terrifying he was in staying committed to his resolutions. You will conclude that the King of England's former frivolities were like the slow-wittedness of the Roman Lucius Junius Brutus, who faked being slow-witted in order to lull the tyrant Lucius Tarquinius Superbus and his son into not fearing him. The ruse worked, and Brutus — the name means 'Dullard' — drove them out of Rome. Brutus covered his intelligence with a coat of folly; this is similar to gardeners spreading manure over the ground in which are planted the flowers that bloom earliest and are the most beautiful."

"I disagree, my lord High Constable," the Dauphin said, "but although I disagree it does not matter. In cases of defense, it is best to believe that enemy is mightier and more powerful than he seems. By doing that, we will ensure that forces required for defense are sufficient. If we were to underestimate the enemy, we might not be able to defend ourselves against him; we would be like a miser who ruins his new coat by not giving his tailor enough cloth to make a good coat."

The King of France said, "We believe that King Harry and his army are strong; therefore, Princes, make sure that you strongly arm to meet him on the battlefield. When training a hawk or hound to kill game animals, it is traditional to flesh the hawk or hound — to give it some of the meat of the game it hunted and killed. Henry V's relatives have earlier been fleshed upon French soldiers. Henry V has been bred out of that bloody race who persistently pursued us in our native paths. For evidence, remember our too-much-memorable shame when at Créssy, Edward the Black Prince of Wales — a black name! — killed and killed again and took captive all our Princes. The Black Prince's father, King Edward III, immovable as a mountain, stood on a mountain high in the air, crowned with the golden Sun, and watched the heroic actions of his son and smiled as he watched him mangle and deface and cut to pieces 20-year-old French soldiers — the work of nature and God and French fathers. Henry V is a branch of that victorious family; therefore, let us fear his natural mightiness and destiny."

A messenger entered the room and said, "Ambassadors from Harry, King of England, request to be admitted into your majesty's presence."

"We will see them immediately," the King of France said. "Go, and bring them here."

The messenger and some lords exited.

The King of France said, "It is as if we are being hunted by Henry V. He is eagerly chasing us."

The Dauphin said, "We should not turn tail and run away; instead, let us turn head and face the enemy. Cowardly dogs bark the loudest — they most spend their mouths — when what they seem to threaten is running far ahead of them. My good sovereign, give the English ambassadors short shrift — treat them curtly. Let them know of what kind of a Monarchy you are the head. Self-love, aka pride, my liege, is not so vile a sin as self-neglecting. Have pride, and do not undervalue yourself."

The French lords reentered the room with the English ambassador — Exeter — and his attendants.

The King of France asked, "Have you come from our brother the King of England?"

Of course, the two Kings were not literally brothers; this was simply a polite way of referring to another King.

"Yes, we have come from him," Exeter said, "and he greets your majesty by desiring you, in the name of God Almighty, to divest yourself and lay aside the borrowed glories that by gift of Heaven, by law of nature, and by the law of nations — that is, by all laws, whether divine, natural, or human — belong to him and to his heirs. Namely, he desires you to divest yourself of and lay aside the crown of France and all the far-reaching honors and titles that pertain by customs and by laws to the crown of France. That you may know that this is no irregular or illegitimate claim that has been fraudulently picked out of old, worm-eaten books or searched out — as with a rake — from the dust of long-forgotten manuscripts or dredged up with bad faith and technicalities, he sends you this very memorable family tree in which his ancestors are listed."

He handed the King of France a document, and then he added, "King Henry V's direct line of descent from King Philip III of France and from King Edward III of England is very clearly shown. When you have looked over this document and seen his ancestry, he directs you then to resign your crown and Kingdom. You hold them fraudulently and are keeping them from him, the natural — by right of birth — and true challenger."

The King of France asked, "What happens if I do not resign my crown and Kingdom?"

"War and blood will happen," Exeter said. "Even if you were to hide the crown in your heart, Henry V will search for it there. To gain his rightful crown he is coming in fierce tempest, in thunder, and in earthquake, like a Jove, the Roman King of the gods. If politely requesting the crown fails to get him the crown, then he will take it by force, and so he asks you, in all compassion, to give him his crown and to take mercy on the poor souls against whom this hungry war will open its vast jaws. On your head will fall the responsibility for the widows' tears for dead husbands, the orphans' cries for dead fathers, the pining maidens' groans for their dead betrothed lovers, and for the dead men's blood that war shall swallow in this dispute. This is his claim, his threatening, and all of my message to you, but if the Dauphin is in the Presence Chamber here, I also have a message especially for him."

The King of France said, "As for us, we will consider this matter further. Tomorrow you shall bear our full reply back to our brother the King of England."

The Dauphin said, "As for the Dauphin, I stand here for him. What is the message you bring for him from the King of England?"

Exeter replied, "The King of England sends the Dauphin scorn and defiance, slight regard, contempt, and anything that is negative yet does not reflect badly on him, the mighty sender; this is how little he values you. Thus says my King, and he adds that if your father the King of France does not grant all his demands in full and thereby sweeten the bitter mock — the joke of tennis balls — you sent his majesty, he will call you to so hot an answer for it that caves and womb-like vaulted passages of France shall chide your trespass and return your mockery by echoing with the sound of his cannon."

"Tell King Henry V that if my father sends him a fair reply, it is against my will," the Dauphin said, "for I desire nothing but conflict with England. For that purpose, and because it was an appropriate gift — because it matched his youth and vanity — I presented him with the Parisian tennis balls."

Exeter replied, "Because of your gift to him, Henry V will make your Parisian royal palace — the Louvre — shake, as he would even if it were the foremost palace — or tennis court — in all of Europe. Be assured that you will find a difference, as we his subjects have in wonder found, between the lack of promise that he showed in his greener, younger, and immature days and the great promise that he has mastered now. Now he uses his time wisely, even to the last second, and you will learn that this is true by studying your own losses, if Henry V stays with his army in France."

The King of France replied, "Tomorrow you shall know in full what we have decided."

Exeter said, "Send us back to Henry V quickly lest he come here himself to find out the reason for our delay — he has already landed on French soil."

"You shall soon be sent back to him with our reply and reasonable terms for peace. A night is only a small pause and a short delay when it comes to forming replies of this importance."

CHAPTER 3

Prologue

The Chorus walked onto stage and said, "Thus with wings of the imagination our swift scene flies in motion of no less velocity than that of thought.

"Imagine that you have seen the well-equipped King of England at Southampton pier go onboard ship and resemble the young Sun-god as the King sails with his fleet with their streaming silken banners. Use your imagination, and you will see ship-boys climbing on ropes made of hemp. You will hear the shrill whistle that gives orders and brings order to the noisy confusion. You will see the sails, moving with the invisible and creeping wind, draw the huge hulls of the ships through the furrowed sea, breasting the lofty surge.

"Imagine that you are standing upon the shore and seeing a city dancing on the inconstant billows because this majestic fleet appears to be a city headed directly for Harfleur, a port in northern France. Follow the ships, follow them. Fix as with grapping irons your minds to the sterns of this navy, and leave your England, as deadly still as at midnight, guarded by grandsires, babies, and old women, all of whom are either past or not arrived at bodily strength and power. What male with a chin that is enriched with even one visible hair will not follow these hand-picked and specially selected Knights to France?

"Work, work your thoughts, and in your minds see a siege; look at the cannons mounted on their frames, with their fatal mouths open and pointing at walled and fortified and besieged Harfleur.

"Now imagine that the ambassador Exeter comes back from the French King and tells Harry that the King offers him his daughter Katherine, and with her, for a dowry, some petty and unprofitable Dukedoms. The offer displeases Henry V, and so the nimble gunner touches the Devilish cannon with a lighted match—"

The sound of a cannon is heard.

"— and part of the French wall collapses.

"Always, members of the audience, be kind, and add to our performance with your mind."

— 3.1 —

At Harfleur, King Henry V was rallying his troops, who had retreated from an assault upon the breach in the wall but were regrouping. With Henry V were Exeter, Bedford, and Gloucester. Some of the soldiers present carried scaling-ladders that would help them climb over the wall.

King Henry V said, "Once more unto the breach, dear friends, once more. Let us attack again and burst through and over the wall or let us close the breach in the wall with the corpses of English soldiers. In peacetime nothing so becomes a man as modest quietness and humility. But when the blast of war blows in our ears, then we ought to imitate the action of the fierce tiger; we should stiffen our sinews, summon up our red blood and courage, disguise our handsome features with hard-featured rage. So let us now glare with our eyes through the portholes of our head like the brass cannon of warships. Let our brows hang over our eyes as fearsomely as a cliff juts out over its eroding base that is violently washed by the wild and wasteful ocean. Now let us set our teeth and flare our nostrils wide, hold hard our breath and bend up our spirit to its full height.

"Fight on, you noblest of the English whose blood is inherited from fathers who have proven themselves in war — fathers who, like so many great Alexanders who conquered the world and mourned that nothing was left to conquer.

"Fight on, you nobles whose fathers fought on French soil from morning until evening and sheathed their swords only when no one was left to oppose them. Do not dishonor your mothers by making it possible for the enemy to say that your mothers cuckolded your fathers; prove by your brave fighting here that those whom you call fathers did in fact beget you. Be examples now to men of grosser blood and teach them how to fight in war.

"And you, good yeomen, you who farm your own land, whose limbs were made in England, show us here the mettle of your pasture and the quality of the country in which you were born. Let us swear that you are worth your breeding, which I do not doubt, because none of you is so humble and lowly by birth that you do not have noble luster in your eyes. I see you stand like greyhounds held back by the leash, straining against the leash in anticipation of the moment it is let loose and you can hunt your prey.

"The game is afoot — seek your prey! Follow your spirit, and as we charge cry, 'God for Harry, England, and Saint George, the patron saint of England!'"

They charged.

— 3.2 —

Nym, Bardolph, Pistol, and the boy who was their servant were at Harfleur.

Bardolph cried, "Charge! Charge! To the breach! To the breach!"

Nym objected, "Please, Corporal, wait. The blows of battle are too severe and dangerous. Speaking for myself, I do not have a pair of lives, but only one. The heat of this battle is too hot — this is plainly true and without ornamentation, just like a plain-song is the plain, simple melody without fancy variations."

Bardolph, formerly a Lieutenant, had been demoted to Corporal.

Pistol said, "The use of 'plain-song' is a most just."

He meant a *mot juste*, French for "exactly the right word."

He added, "The plain truth is that the blows of battle abound in this battle."

He sang, "*Blows come and go; God's servants drop and die; and sword and shield, in this bloody field, do win immortal fame.*"

The boy said, "I wish that I were in an alehouse in London! I would trade all my chances for fame and glory for a pot of ale and safety."

Pistol said, "So would I."

He sang, "*If wishes would prevail with me,*

"*My purpose — my desire for ale — should not fail with me,*

"*But thither — to an alehouse — would I hurry.*"

Pistol's singing voice was poor, and his desire to stay out of the battle was dishonorable.

The boy sang in answer to Pistol, "*You sing as surely and as honorably, but not as well, as a bird without honor sings on a bough.*"

On his horse, Fluellen, a Welsh Captain serving Henry V, came toward Nym, Bardolph, and Pistol, outraged that they were not fighting in the battle. The boy was too young to fight, but he was supposed to stay in the English camp and guard the tents.

Fluellen shouted, "Up to the breach, you dogs! Hurry, you gonads!"

Fluellen drove Nym, Bardolph, and Pistol forward.

Moving forward as slowly as Fluellen would allow him, Pistol pleaded, "Be merciful, great Duke, to men of mold. We are made of clay, just as the Bible says. Abate your rage, abate your manly rage — abate your rage, great Duke!"

As he did so frequently, Pistol was using his poor knowledge of Latin poorly. By "Duke," he meant *Dux*, which is Latin for "leader."

Pistol continued to plead, "Good and fine fellow, abate your rage; be lenient, good lad!"

Nym said to Fluellen, "This is a poor change of mood! We were in a good mood, but you are putting us in a bad mood!"

Fluellen used his whip to make the three men race to the front, leaving the boy behind.

The boy said to himself, "As young as I am, I have closely observed these three swashers and swaggerers: Nym, Bardolph, and Pistol. I am boy — that is, a young servant — to all three of them, but all three of them, if they should ever serve me, could not be man — a grown-up male servant — to me because all these three clowns put together do not amount to a single man.

"As for Bardolph, he is white-livered and red-faced — he is a cowardly alcoholic. Because he has a red face, people think that he is hot-tempered, and so he outfaces his opponents in battles and quarrels, but he does not fight. He prefers to act like a fighter rather than actually fight.

"As for Pistol, he has a killing tongue and a quiet, peaceful sword. He prefers to brag big and fight not even a little. He breaks his words, and he keeps his weapons whole. The battles he fights are verbal, and he does not keep his promises, and his sword is never broken because he does not use it in battle.

"As for Nym, he has heard that men of few words are the best men; he has heard the proverb *vir sapit qui pauca loquitur* — 'a wise man is one who does not talk much.' Therefore, Nym is scornful of and does not say his prayers, lest he should be thought a coward. However, his few bad words are matched with his few good deeds and deeds of valor. He never broke any man's head but his own, and that was against a post when he was drunk.

"These three men will steal anything, and call it a purchase. Bardolph stole a lute-case, carried it for 36 English miles, and then sold it for a penny and a half. Nym and Bardolph are sworn brothers in filching, aka stealing, and in town they stole a fire shovel. I knew by that piece of work that the men would carry coals. 'To carry coals' is figurative language for to do degrading, humiliating, and insulting work and to submit to degrading, humiliating, and insulting treatment.

"They would have me as familiar with men's pockets as the men's gloves or handkerchiefs. They want me to become a pickpocket and become familiar with the inside of other people's pockets. This goes much against my sense of what it is to be a man. If I should take something from another person's pocket so that I can put it into my pocket, it would be a plain pocketing up of wrong. 'To pocket up wrongs' is figurative language for to be guilty of stealing and to submit to insults — such as being called a thief. I must leave these three men and seek some better service with some better men. These three men's villainy goes against my weak stomach, and therefore I must throw it — my job and the contents of my stomach — up."

The boy returned to the English camp.

Meanwhile, Fluellen and Gower, who was an English Captain, were talking. Fluellen, the Welsh Captain, had a heavy accent. He sometimes pronounced the letter *b* like the letter *p*, the letter *f* like the letter *v*, and the letter *j* like the letters *ch*. He also tended to use fancy words, frequently use synonyms, and repeat the unnecessary phrase "look you." The Irish Captain, Macmorris, and the Scottish Captain, Jamy, also had heavy accents.

Captain Gower had been searching for Fluellen. Having found him, he said, "Captain Fluellen, you must come immediately to the tunnels that we are building under the besieged city's walls so that we can use explosives to blow them up. The Duke of Gloucester needs to speak with you."

"You want me to go to the tunnels!" Fluellen said. "Tell the Duke that it is not so good for me to come to the tunnels because, look you, the tunnels have not been constructed according to the disciplines of the war: The concavities [hollowness] of the tunnels are not sufficient [good enough], for, look you, the athversary [adversary], you may discuss this with the Duke, look you, has himself dug tunnels four yards underneath the tunnels we have dug. By Cheshu [Jesu, aka Jesus], I think he will plow [blow] up all our tunnels, if better orders are not given."

Captain Gower replied, "The Duke of Gloucester, to whom the plan of action of the siege has been given, is being advised by an Irishman who is truly a very valiant gentleman."

"He is Captain Macmorris, isn't he?"

"I think that is him."

"By Cheshu [Jesu, aka Jesus], he is an ass, as much an ass as any ass in the world. I will verify as much in his beard [I will tell him that to his face]. He has no more directions in [knowledge of] the true disciplines of the wars, of the Roman disciplines, look you, than does a puppydog."

Captain Macmorris, the Irish Captain, accompanied by Jamy, the Scottish Captain, rode up on their horses.

Captain Gower said, "Here he comes; and the Scots Captain, Jamy, is with him."

Captain Fluellen said, "Captain Jamy is a marvelous falourous [valorous] gentleman, that is certain; and he is of great expedition [quick action] and has great knowledge of the aunchient [ancient] wars, as I know from my particular and personal knowledge of his orders. By Cheshu, he will maintain his argument [keep up his part in a discussion] in a conversation about the disciplines of the pristine [flawless and perfectly executed, and ancient] wars of the Romans as well as any military man in the world."

Captain Jamy, the Scottish Captain, said, "I say gud-day [good day], Captain Fluellen."

Captain Fluellen replied, "God-den [Good evening] to your worship, good Captain James."

Captain Gower asked, "How are you, Captain Macmorris! Have you quit the digging of the tunnels? Have the pioneers — the diggers of the tunnels — stopped their work?"

Captain Macmorris replied, "By Chrish [Christ], la! T'ish [It is] ill done: the work ish give over [is given up], the trompet [trumpet] sounds the order to retreat. By my hand, I swear, and by my father's soul, the work ish [is] ill done; it ish give over [we have given it up]. If the trumpet had not sounded the order to retreat, I would have blowed [blown] up the town, so Chrish save me — la! — in an hour. Oh, t'ish ill done! T'ish ill done; I swear by my hand, t'ish ill done!"

Captain Fluellen said, "Captain Macmorris, I beg you now, will you voutsafe [vouchsafe, aka grant] me, look you, a few disputations [discussions] with you, as partly touching [regarding] or concerning the disciplines of the war, the Roman wars, in the way of argument, look you, and friendly communication; partly to satisfy my opinion, and partly for the satisfaction, look you, of my mind, as touching the direction of the military discipline; that is the point."

Captain Jamy, the Scot, said, "It sall [shall] be vary gud [very good], in gud faith [in good faith, aka truly], gud [good] Captains bath [both]: and I sall 'quit [shall requite, aka answer] you with gud leve [with good leave, aka with your permission], as I may pick occasion [as I have the opportunity] that sall [shall] I, marry [by Mother Mary]."

Captain Macmorris said, "It is no time to discourse [This is not a time for conversation], so Chrish [Christ] save me: The day is hot, and the weather, and the wars, and the King, and the Dukes, everyone is busy fighting, and it is no time to discourse. The town is beseeched [besieged], and now the trumpet calls on us to go on attack at the breach; and we talk, and, by Chrish [Christ], we do nothing. It is a shame for us all, so God sa' [save] me, it is a shame to stand still; it is a shame, I swear by my hand because there are throats to be cut, and works to be done; and there ish [is] nothing done, so Chrish sa' [save] me, la!"

Captain Jamy said, "By the mess [Mass], ere theise [before these] eyes of mine take themselves to slomber [slumber; that is, before I go to sleep tonight] ay'll [I'll] do gud [good] service, or ay'll lie i' the grund for it [or I'll lie in my grave]. Ay [I] owe Got [God] a death; and ay'll [I'll] pay it as valorously as I can, that sall [shall] I surely do, that is the breff [brief] and the long [aka the long and the short of it]. Marry [By Mother Mary], I wad full fain hear [I would very much like to hear] some question [discussion] between you tway [two]."

Captain Fluellen said, "Captain Macmorris, I think, look you, under your correction [correct me if I'm wrong], there are not many of your nation —"

Captain Macmorris was quick to take offense, and he misunderstood Fluellen and took offense too quickly as Fluellen had said nothing wrong: "Of my nation! What ish [is] my nation? Ish [You are] a villain, and a bastard, and a knave, and a rascal. What ish [is] my nation? Who talks of [about] my nation?"

Captain Fluellen replied, "Look you, if you take the matter otherwise than is meant, Captain Macmorris, peradventure [perhaps] I shall think you do not use [treat] me with that affability as in discretion you ought to use [treat] me, look you, since I am as good a man as yourself, both in the disciplines of war, and in the derivation of my birth, and in other particularities."

Captain Macmorris said, "I do not know that you are so good a man as myself. Chrish [Christ] save me, I will cut off your head."

Captain Gower said, "Gentlemen, both of you are misunderstanding each other."

Captain Jamy said, "A! [Aye! aka Yes!] That's a foul fault."

A trumpet sounded, blowing the notes for a parley — a meeting between the leaders of the opposing forces.

Captain Gower said, "That is a trumpet from the town. The leader of Harfleur has ordered a trumpeter to sound a parley."

Captain Fluellen said, "Captain Macmorris, when there is more better opportunity to be required [when a better time presents itself], look you, I will be so bold as to tell you I know the disciplines of war; and there is an end."

— 3.3 —

The Governor of Harfleur and some citizens of the town stood on the gates. Below them, in front of the gates, stood King Henry V and his soldiers.

King Henry V asked, "What have you, the Governor of Harfleur, resolved to do? This is the last parle we will agree to, so either surrender or fight. Surrender, and hand yourselves over to our best mercy, or like men excited by destructive war the way that a bitch is excited when she is in heat, defy us and tell us to do our worst. I swear that as I am a soldier — a name that I think becomes me best — if I begin the assaults against your town once again, I will not leave the half-conquered Harfleur until she lies buried in the ashes of her buildings. The gates of my mercy shall be all shut up, and my soldiers, rough and hard of heart and having already tasted your blood, with complete freedom given to their bloody hands shall go throughout your town with consciences that can commit any deed applauded in Hell, and shall mow down your fresh, fair virgins and your flowering, growing infants.

"If you continue to fight me, then what is it to me if civil war — a war in which you fight your rightful King — arrayed in flames like the Prince of Fiends, Lucifer, and with his complexion begrimed by smoke from the firing of gunpowder, results in all manner of deadly feats linked together with waste and desolation?

"If you continue to fight me, then what is it to me, when you yourselves are the cause of all the evil deeds that will make you victims, if your pure maidens fall into the hands of soldiers who will eagerly and violently rape them?

"What reins can stop licentious wickedness when it fiercely gallops down a steep hill? We may as uselessly give our vain commands to the enraged soldiers

49

as they rape and murder and loot as send an order to the sea-monster Leviathan to come ashore. Our enraged soldiers busily engaged in the act of sacking your city will obey my commands just as much as will the whale Leviathan.

"Therefore, you men of Harfleur, take pity on your town and on your people, while my soldiers still obey my commands, and while the cool and temperate wind of human kindness still blows away the filthy and contagious clouds of intoxicating murder, spoil, and villainy.

"If you will not take pity on your town and on your people, why, in a moment look to see the reckless and blind-to-mercy bloody soldiers with their foul hands defile the locks of your shrill-shrieking daughters as they drag them away to be raped. Look to see the reckless and bloody soldiers with their foul hands take your fathers by their silver beards and dash their most reverend heads against the walls. Look to see your naked infants spitted upon pikes as if they were to be roasted in a fireplace while their mad mothers with their confused howls scream into the clouds as their tears fall like a cloudburst just like the Jewish mothers did when Herod's bloody-hunting slaughtermen killed all the Jewish boys who were two years old or younger.

"What do you say? Will you surrender, and avoid rape, murder, the deaths of infants, and looting, or — guilty because you defend yourselves against your rightful King — be destroyed?"

The Governor of Harfleur replied, "Our hopes have this day come to an end. The Dauphin, from whom we entreated armies to relieve us, has sent us a message that his armies are not yet ready to raise a siege as great as this. Therefore, great King, we surrender our town and lives to your soft mercy.

"Enter our gates, and do what you want with us and what and who are ours, for we are no longer capable of mounting a defense."

Henry V ordered, "Open your gates."

Some citizens of Harfleur began to open the gates.

Henry V then said, "Uncle Exeter, go and enter Harfleur; there remain, and fortify it strongly against the French. Show mercy to all the citizens of Harfleur. As for us, dear uncle, winter is coming on and many of our soldiers are suffering from sickness. Therefore, we will march to Calais, a seaport in France under our control. Tonight in Harfleur we will be your guest; tomorrow we will begin the march."

The gates now open, King Henry V, Exeter, and the English army entered Harfleur.

$$— 3.4 —$$

The French had suffered a major defeat when Harfleur fell.

Katherine had been offered as a bride to Henry V, along with some Dukedoms, earlier, but the English King had rejected the offer and had invaded France. Now it looked as if Katherine might still marry Henry V and that he might become the King of France. Katherine decided to start learning English in a room of the French palace with the help of Alice, a gentlewoman who was somewhat older than she.

Katherine said, "*Alice, tu as ete en Angleterre, et tu parles bien le langage.*"

[Katherine said, "Alice, you have been in England, and you know the language well."]

Alice replied, "*Un peu, madame.*"

[Alice replied, "A little, madame."]

Katherine said, "*Je te prie, m'enseignez: il faut que j'apprenne a parler. Comment appelez-vous la main en Anglois?*"

[Katherine said, "Please, teach me the language. I need to learn it. What is the English for *la main*?]

Alice replied, "*La main? Elle est appelee* de hand."

[Alice replied, "*La main?* It is called de hand."]

Katherine said, "De hand. *Et les doigts?*"

[Katherine said, "De hand. And the fingers?"]

Alice replied, "*Les doigts? Ma foi, j'oublie les doigts; mais je me souviendrai. Les doigts? Je pense qu'ils sont appeles* de fingres; *oui, del.*"

[Alice replied, "*Les doigts?* By my faith, I have forgotten the English for *les doigts*, but I will remember. I think that they are called de fingres; yes, de fingres."]

Katherine said, "*La main,* de hand; *les doigts,* de fingres. *Je pense que je suis le bon ecolier; j'ai gagne deux mots d'Anglois vitement. Comment appelez-vous les ongles?*"

[Katherine said, "*La main* is de hand; *les doigts* is de fingres. I think that I am a good scholar; I have learned already two words of English. What do you call *les ongles*?"]

Alice replied, "*Les ongles? Nous les appelons* de nails."

[Alice replied, "*Les ongles?* We call them de nails."]

Katherine said, "De nails. *Ecoutez; dites-moi, si je parle bien*: de hand, de fingres, *et* de nails."

[Katherine said, "De nails. Listen, and tell me if I am speaking correctly: de hand, de fingres, and de nails."]

Alice replied, "*C'est bien dit, madame; il est fort bon Anglois.*"

[Alice replied, "It is well said, madame; it is very good English."]

Katherine said, "*Dites-moi l'Anglois pour le bras.*"

[Katherine said, "Tell me what is the English for *le bras.*"]

Alice replied, "De arm, madame."

Katherine asked, "*Et* [And] *le coude?*"

Alice replied, "De elbow."

Katherine said, "De elbow. *Je m'en fais la repetition de tous les mots que vous m'avez appris des a present.*"

[Katherine said, "De elbow. I will now repeat all the words you have taught me up until the present."]

Alice replied, "*Il est trop difficile, madame, comme je pense.*"

[Alice replied, "That is too difficult, madame, I think."]

Katherine replied, "*Excusez-moi, Alice; ecoutez*: de hand, de fingres, de nails, de arma, de bilbow."

[Katherine replied, "Excuse me, Alice, but you are wrong. Listen: de hand, de fingres, de nails, de arma, de bilbow."]

Alice said, "De elbow, madame."

Katherine said, "*O, Seigneur Dieu, je m'en oublie*! De elbow. *Comment appelez-vous le col?*"

[Katherine said, "Oh, Lord God, I forgot! De elbow. What do you call *le col?*]

Alice replied, "De neck, madame."

Katherine said, "De nick. *Et le menton?*"

Alice replied, "De chin."

Katherine said, "De sin. *Le col* is de nick; de *menton* is de sin."

Alice replied, "*Oui. Sauf votre honneur, en verite, vous prononcez les mots aussi droit que les natifs d'Angleterre.*"

[Alice replied, "Yes. Saving your reverence, truly you pronounce the words as straight as do the natives of England."]

Katherine said, "*Je ne doute point d'apprendre, par la grace de Dieu, et en peu de temps.*"

[Katherine said, "I have no doubt that I shall learn English, by the grace of God, and in only a short time."]

Alice asked, "*N'avez vous pas deja oublie ce que je vous ai enseigne?*"

[Alice asked, "Haven't you already forgotten what I taught you?"]

Katherine replied, "*Non, je reciterai a vous promptement*: de hand, de fingres, de mails —"

[Katherine replied, "No, I shall repeat it for you right now: de hand, de fingres, de mails —"]

Alice said, "De nails, madame."

Katherine said, "De nails, de arm, de ilbow."

Alice said, "*Sauf votre honneur*, de elbow."

[Alice said, "If it please your honor, de elbow."]

Katherine said, "*Ainsi dis-je*: de elbow, de nick, *et* de sin. *Comment appelez-vous le pied et la robe?*"

[Katherine said, "That's what I said: de elbow, de nick, and de sin. What do you call *le pied* and *la robe*?"]

Alice replied, "De foot, madame; *et* [and] de coun."

This shocked Katherine. The English word "foot" sounds similar to the French word "*foutre*," which means "f**k." Alice's word "coun," by which she meant the English word "gown," sounds similar to the French word "*con*," which means "c*nt."

Katherine said, "De foot *et* de coun! *O Seigneur Dieu! ce sont mots de son mauvais, corruptible, gros, et impudique, et non pour les dames d'honneur d'user: je ne voudrais prononcer ces mots devant les seigneurs de France pour tout le monde. Foh!* Le foot *et* le coun! *Neanmoins, je reciterai une autre fois ma lecon ensemble*: de hand, de fingres, de nails, de arm, de elbow, de nick, de sin, de foot, de coun."

[Katherine said, "De foot and de coun! Oh, Lord God! These words are evil, corrupting, gross, and shameless, and not for an honorable lady to use! I would not say these words in front of French gentlemen for the entire world. Oh! Le foot and le coun! Nevertheless, I will recite all of my lesson again: de hand, de fingres, de nails, de arm, de elbow, de nick, de sin, de foot, de coun."]

Alice said, "Excellent, madame!"

Katherine replied, "*C'est assez pour une fois. Allons-nous a diner.*"

[Katherine replied, "That is enough for one lesson. Let's go to dinner."]

— 3.5 —

In a room of the French palace, the King of France, his son the Dauphin, the Duke of Bourbon, the Constable of France, and other high-ranking officials were meeting to discuss King Henry V's victory at Harfleur and his tactical withdrawal to Calais.

The King of France said, "It is certain that he has passed the Somme River."

The Somme River is halfway between Harfleur and Calais.

The Constable said, "If we don't fight him, my lord, let us not live in France; let us all give up and give our vineyards to a barbarous people."

The Dauphin said, "*Oh, Dieu vivant*! [Oh, living God!] These Englishmen are a few sprays — offshoots and ejaculations — of us French. They shot up from what our fathers emptied out of their lustful bodies when they — our Norman ancestors — invaded and conquered England in 1066. These Englishmen are our ancestors' scions — they are sprigs that were grafted onto wild and savage stock. Shall they shoot up so suddenly into the clouds and look down on us, who are descended from the people who grafted them?"

Bourbon said, "They are Normans, they are only the bastards of the Normans who conquered them and then slept with their women, they are Norman bastards! *Mort de ma vie*! [Death of my life!] If they march along without our engaging them in battle, I will sell my Dukedom and buy a wet and slimy farm in that misshapen isle of Albion, aka England, Scotland, and Wales."

The Constable said, "*Dieu de batailles*! [God of battles!] Where has the English army gotten this courage and spirit? Is not their climate foggy, raw, and dull, and does not the Sun, as if in despite, look pale as it looks down on them and kills their fruit with frowns? Can ale, their barley-broth, which is no better than boiled water, and which is a medicinal drink for hard-ridden horses of inferior breed, infuse and warm up their cold blood to such valiant heat? And shall our quick blood, spirited with wine, seem frosty? Hot blood is courageous blood. Oh, for the honor of our land, let us not be like icicles hanging from our houses' roofs, while a more frosty people are ready to sweat drops of gallant youth in our rich fields of battle! But we should call our fields poor because of the lack of quality in the lords they have bred."

The Dauphin said, "By my faith and honor, our ladies mock us, and plainly say that our spirit has been bred out of us and that therefore they will give their bodies to the lust of English youth to newly restock France with bastard warriors."

Bourbon said, "They tell us to go to the English dancing-schools and teach the high jumps in the lavolta dances and the swift running steps in the coranto dances; they say that our grace is only in our heels, and that we are most lofty runaways — they say that we are nobly born men who swiftly run away from battles."

"Where is Montjoy the herald?" the King of France asked. "Bring him here quickly. Let him greet the King of England with our sharp defiance. Up, Princes, and with your honorable spirit of honor more sharply edged than your swords, hurry to the battlefield! Charles Delabreth, High Constable of France; you Dukes of Orleans, Bourbon, and of Berri, Alençon, Brabant, Bar, and Burgundy; Jaques Chatillon, Rambures, Vaudemont, Beaumont, Grandpré, Roussi, and Fauconberg, Foix, Lestrale, Bouciqualt, and Charolois; high Dukes, great Princes, Barons, lords and Knights, for the sake of your great positions and family-seats, clear yourselves of great shames. Stop Harry England, who sweeps through our land with battle flags and streamers painted with the blood of the French soldiers at Harfleur. Rush against his army just like the melted snow avalanches upon the valleys, whose low vassal seat the Alps spit and empty their phlegm upon. Go against him — you have power enough — defeat and capture him, and bring him as your prisoner in a captive's military carriage to the city of Rouen."

The Constable said, "This command is appropriate for your greatness, King of France. I am sorry that the number of Henry V's soldiers is so few and that his soldiers are sick and famished in their march because I am sure that when Henry V sees our French army, he will drop his heart into his stomach out of fear and offer us a ransom not to attack his army and him."

The King of France replied, "Therefore, Lord Constable, order Montjoy to quickly go and let him say to Harry England that we send to know what ransom he will willingly give to us."

He added, "Prince Dauphin, you shall stay with us in Rouen."

The Dauphin objected, "Please, no, your majesty."

"Be patient, for you shall remain with us," the King of France ordered.

He then ordered, "Now go forth, Constable and all you Princes, and quickly bring us word that Henry V's pride has fallen without a battle or that his army has fallen in battle."

— 3.6 —

In the English camp at Picardy in northern France, Gower, the English Captain, and Fluellen, the Welsh Captain, met and talked about a battle that had occurred when the English soldiers took possession of a bridge over the Ternoise River. The English soldiers needed to cross this bridge on their march to Calais.

Captain Gower said, "How are you, Captain Fluellen! Have you come from the bridge?"

Captain Fluellen replied, "I assure you, there have been very excellent services committed at the bridge."

"Is the Duke of Exeter safe?"

"The Duke of Exeter is as magnanimous and great in heart as Agamemnon, Commander-in-Chief of the Greek soldiers allied to fight the Trojans. Exeter is a man whom I love and honor with my soul, and my heart, and my duty, and my life, and my living, and my uttermost power. He is not — God be praised and blessed! — at all hurt in the world; instead, he keeps the pridge [bridge] most valiantly, with excellent discipline.

"There is an Aunchient [Ancient, aka Ensign] Lieutenant there at the pridge [bridge]. I think in my very conscience that he is as valiant a man as Mark Antony, who after the death of his friend Julius Caesar attempted to seize control of Rome, and he is a man of no estimation or reputation in the world, but I did see him do as gallant service as any soldier."

Captain Gower asked, "What do you call him? What is his name?"

Captain Fluellen replied, "He is called Aunchient Pistol."

"I don't know him."

Pistol now came walking toward the two Captains.

Captain Fluellen said, "Here is the man himself."

Pistol said to Fluellen, "Captain, I beg you to do me a favor. The Duke of Exeter well respects you."

Captain Fluellen replied, "That is true, and I praise God because of it. I have merited and earned some respect from Exeter."

Pistol said, "Bardolph, a soldier, firm and sound of heart, and of vigorous and sturdy valor, has, by cruel fate, and by unstable Fortune's furious fickle wheel ... the wheel of that blind goddess who stands upon the rolling restless stone —"

The goddess Fortune was often shown blindfolded and turning the Wheel of Fortune to determine whether a person's fortune would be good or bad, and was often depicted as standing on a round and rolling stone. Sometimes the goddess Fortune was depicted doing both at the same time.

Captain Fluellen explicated the two images of the goddess Fortune: Excuse me, Aunchient Pistol, for interrupting you. Fortune is painted blind, with a bandage before her eyes, to signify to you that Fortune is blind; and she is painted also with a wheel, to signify to you, which is the moral of it, that she is turning, and inconstant, and mutability, and variation: and her foot, look you, is fixed upon a spherical stone, which rolls, and rolls, and rolls. Truly, the poet makes a most excellent description of it — in a letter written while he was in exile, Ovid wrote about 'the goddess who admits by her unsteady wheel her own fickleness; she always has its apex beneath her swaying foot.' Fortune is an excellent symbolical figure."

Pistol replied, "Fortune is Bardolph's foe, and frowns on him; for he has stolen a pax, and he has been sentenced to be hanged — a damned and shameful death!"

A pax was a religious item: a tablet depicting the Crucifixion. The priest and church members taking communion passed around and kissed the pax. *Pax* is Latin for "peace," and King Henry V had turned the *pax* of England and France into war by invading France.

Pistol continued, "Let gallows gape for dog — dogs are executed for their offences — but let man go free and let not a rope made of hemp suffocate his windpipe. But Exeter has given the doom of death for a pax of little price. Therefore, go and speak to Exeter: The Duke will hear your voice. Do not let Bardolph's vital thread of life be cut with the edge of a hangman's cheap rope and with vile reproach. Speak, Captain, to save Bardolph's life, and I will repay you."

Captain Fluellen was not the type of man to be bribed. He said, "Aunchient Pistol, I do partly understand your meaning."

Pistol's verbose verbiage was difficult to understand — and so was Captain Fluellen's.

"Why, then, let us rejoice therefore. A man's life has been saved."

Captain Fluellen replied, "Not so fast, Aunchient, it is not a thing to rejoice at, because, if, look you, Bardolph were my brother, I would still desire the Duke to use his good pleasure and do what he wants to do, and put him to execution; for discipline ought to be used. I am all for discipline, and King Henry V has made it clear that soldiers are not allowed to loot churches on pain of death."

Angry, Pistol said, "Die and be damned! — and here is something for your friendship!"

Pistol made an obscene gesture with one middle finger.

Captain Fluellen said, "It is well."

Pistol said, "Let me double that!"

Pistol made two obscene gestures with both of his middle fingers and then exited.

Captain Fluellen said, "Very good."

Captain Fluellen believed in discipline, but he was not a hothead and he was not a coward. He had more important things to do than discipline Pistol right now — he had to give Captain Gower and King Henry V news about the bridge. He was also willing to cut Pistol some slack right now because 1) he believed that Pistol had done deeds of courage at the bridge, and 2) Pistol was upset about the soon-to-occur death of a friend. However, at a later time, when the time was right, he would deal with Pistol — no Aunchient should talk that way to a Captain.

Captain Gower recognized Pistol, however, and said, "Why, he is an arrant counterfeit rascal; I remember him now; he is a bawd, aka pimp, and a cutpurse, aka pickpocket."

Captain Fluellen said, "I'll assure you that he uttered as brave words at the bridge as you shall see in a summer's day. But it is very well; what he has spoken to me, that is well, but I tell you, when the time is right —"

Captain Gower interrupted, "Why, he is a stupid oaf, a fool, a rogue, who now and then goes to the wars, to put on airs and magnify himself at his return to London in the guise of a soldier. And such fellows are perfect in memorizing the names of the great commanders. They memorize where battles were fought, at such and such a fortification, at such a breach, with such a military escort; who came off bravely, who was shot, who was disgraced, what terms the enemy accepted; and all this they learn perfectly in military language, which they trick up and embellish with freshly coined oaths. What a beard trimmed like a general's and what some well-worn military clothing will do among foaming bottles and ale-washed wits is wonderful to be thought on. People such as he tell great lies so they can get treated in bars. Captain Fluellen, you must learn to know such slanderers of this age, or else you may be marvelously mistook and believe that a coward is a hero."

Captain Fluellen had been listening closely to Captain Gower, and he believed what Captain Gower had told him about Pistol. True, Pistol had spoken well at the bridge, and at first Captain Fluellen had believed what Pistol had said, but impressive words did not necessarily translate into impressive deeds. Also, he now remembered that Pistol was in a group of three men that he had had to force to go and fight at the breach of the wall of Harfleur.

Captain Fluellen said, "I tell you what, Captain Gower; I do perceive that Pistol is not the man whom he would gladly pretend to the world he is. If I find the right opportunity, I will tell him what I think of him."

They heard the sound of a drum.

Captain Fluellen said, "Listen, the King is coming, and I must speak with him from [about] the pridge [bridge]."

King Henry V, Gloucester, and some soldiers came over to Captain Fluellen and Captain Gower.

Captain Fluellen said, "God pless [bless] your majesty!"

King Henry V said, "How are you, Fluellen! Have you come from the bridge?"

"Ay, so please your majesty. The Duke of Exeter has very gallantly maintained the pridge. The French soldiers have gone off, look you; and there have been gallant and most prave [brave] passages of arms and fighting. By Mother Mary, the athversary [adversaries] had possession of the pridge; but he was forced to retire, and the Duke of Exeter is master of the pridge. I can tell your majesty that the Duke is a prave man."

"What men have you lost, Fluellen?" King Henry V asked.

"The perdition of the athversary [adversary] has been very great, reasonably great, by Mother Mary, but as far as I know, I think that the Duke has lost not a single man, except for one who is likely to be executed for robbing a church, one Bardolph, if your majesty know the man. You may remember seeing him: His face is all bubukles [abcessed carbuncles; Fluellen had combined words meaning "abscess" and "carbuncle"], and pistules and pimples, and knobs, and flames of fire, and his lips blows at his nose [his lower lip jutted out and his breath was like a bellows inflaming his nose], and it is like a coal of fire, sometimes plue [blue] and sometimes red; but by now his nose is executed and his fire's out."

Of course, although Captain Fluellen did not know it, King Henry V knew Bardolph from before he became King; Bardolph had been one of his low-life friends in Eastcheap.

Henry V said, "We would have the breath of all such offenders so cut off. We give express orders that in our marches through the country that there be nothing taken by force from the villages, nothing taken except what is paid for, and none of the French upbraided or abused in disdainful language because when lenity and cruelty play for a Kingdom, the gentler gambler is the soonest winner."

A trumpet announced the arrival of Montjoy, the herald sent by the King of France to deliver a message to King Henry V.

A distinctive trumpet call sounded, and Montjoy came over to Henry V. Montjoy was wearing the distinctive clothing — a tabard coat emblazoned with the arms of the King of the France — that identified him as the King of France's herald. As a herald, Montjoy could not be ethically harmed by his enemy.

Montjoy said, "You know who I am by my tabard coat."

Henry V replied, "Well, then, I know you. What shall I learn from you?"

Montjoy replied, "My master's mind."

"Reveal it."

"Thus says my King," Montjoy said. "Say you to Harry of England: Though we seemed dead, we only slept. Advantage is a better soldier than rashness: He was rash to invade France, but now we have the advantage of him. Tell him we could have rebuked him at Harfleur, but that we thought it was not good to squeeze the pus from an abscess before the right time. Now is the right time. We speak now, and our voice is imperial. The King of England shall repent his folly, see his weakness, and wonder at our patience. Bid him therefore consider what ransom he can offer us in payment of the injuries that he has inflicted on France. This ransom must be in proportion to the losses we have borne, the subjects we have lost, and the disgrace we have digested and endured. To make complete compensation for these injuries, the ransom would weigh so much that his weak pettiness would bow under the heavy load. For our losses, his entire wealth is too poor; for the shedding of our blood, the entire roll call of the soldiers of his Kingdom too small a number; and for our disgrace, his own person, kneeling at our feet, would be only a weak and worthless satisfaction. To this, add defiance, and tell him, in conclusion, that he has betrayed his followers, whose condemnation is pronounced. So says my King and master; I have performed my duty in telling you his words."

King Henry V answered, "What is your name? I know your profession and ability."

"Montjoy."

"You do your office fairly and well," Henry V said. "Go back to your King and tell him that I do not seek him now to fight him. Instead, I prefer to march on to Calais without any opposition. To say the truth, although it is not wise to confess so much to a crafty enemy who has the advantage over us, my soldiers are much enfeebled because of sickness, the numbers of my soldiers are greatly lessened because of battles and disease, and those few soldiers I have are almost no better than so many French. But when my soldiers were healthy, I tell you, herald, I thought one pair of English legs could defeat in battle three pairs of French legs. But, forgive me, God, for bragging like this! Your air of France and your heir of the King of France have blown that vice of bragging into me, as it has into all Frenchmen. I must repent.

"Go, therefore, and tell your master that here I am; my ransom is this frail and worthless trunk that is my body — I do not offer him a trunk that is filled with treasure. My army is only a weak and sickly guard. But tell your King that we will continue on our way with God leading us, even if the King of France himself and another neighbor just like him stand in our way."

Henry V gave Montjoy some money, as was traditional, and said, "There's for your labor, Montjoy. Go tell your master to consider matters carefully. If we may continue our journey without opposition, we will; but if your army hinders us, we shall discolor your tawny ground with your red blood.

"Therefore, Montjoy, fare you well. The sum of all our answer is only this: As we are, we will not seek a battle; nor, as we are, we will not shun it. Tell your master this."

"I will tell him. Thanks to your highness."

Montjoy exited.

The Duke of Gloucester, Henry V's brother, said to him, "I hope they will not come after us and battle us now."

"We are in God's hand, brother, not in theirs," Henry V said. "We will march to the bridge; it is nearing night. Tonight beyond the river we and our army will camp, and tomorrow we will march away."

— 3.7 —

At the French camp, near Agincourt, the Constable of France, the Lord Rambures, Orleans, the Dauphin, and others were talking. In the morning they would fight the English army in the Battle of Agincourt on that day of 25 October 1415. The French vastly outnumbered the English, and the French were confident — make that overconfident — of victory, and they were joking with and insulting each other.

The Constable said in the middle of a discussion about armor and horses, "Ha! I have the best armor in the world. I wish it were morning so that we could begin the battle!"

Orleans said, "You have excellent armor, but give my horse his due."

The Constable said, "It is the best horse of Europe."

"Will it never be morning?" Orleans complained.

The Dauphin said, "My Lord of Orleans, and my lord High Constable, are you talking about horses and suits of armor?"

Orleans replied, "You are as well provided with both as any Prince in the world."

"What a long night is this!" the Dauphin complained. "I would not exchange my horse for any that treads the earth on four legs. Ha! My horse bounds from the earth, as if his entrails were as light as hairs. What horse do I have? *Le cheval volant* [The flying horse], the Pegasus, who flew *chez les narines de feu* [in the nostrils of fire]! He flew bearing a hero to battle the fire-breathing Chimera. When I bestride him, I soar and I am a hawk. He trots the air; the earth sings when he touches it; the basest horn of his hoof is more musical than

ne pipe of Hermes. My horse runs quickly and seldom touches the earth; when
does touch the earth, its hoofs create a musical sound."

Pegasus was a winged horse that came into existence when the ancient
Greek hero Perseus cut off the head of Medusa, a Gorgon. Medusa's blood
pouted, and Pegasus came into existence from that blood.

Orleans said, "He's of the color of the nutmeg: brown."

The Dauphin added, "And of the heat of the ginger. My horse is a beast for
Perseus. My horse is made of the purer, nobler elements of air and fire; and the
fuller and baser elements of earth and water never appear in him, except when
he touches the earth patiently and stilly while his rider mounts him. My horse
indeed a horse, and all other jades you may call beasts."

The Dauphin was not good with words. He had just said that his horse was
not affected by the baser elements except when he — the Dauphin — mounted
him. The Dauphin had also implied that his horse was better than he was, and
he had said that his horse was a jade — a nag.

The Constable said, "Indeed, my lord, it is a most absolute and excellent
horse."

The Dauphin said, "It is the Prince of palfreys; his neigh is like the bidding
of a Monarch and his countenance enforces homage."

Again, the Dauphin had not spoken well. If his horse was the Prince of
palfreys, it was the best of palfreys, but a palfrey was not a battle horse — it was
smaller, lighter horse, the kind that was often ridden by ladies.

Aware that the Dauphin was unknowingly making a fool of himself,
Orleans said, "Speak no more, cousin."

"No," the Dauphin replied, "a man has no wit if he cannot, from the rising
of the lark in the morning to the taking of shelter by the lamb at night, state
varied and deserved praise on my palfrey. It is a theme as fluent and flowing
as the sea. It can turn each grain of sand into an eloquent speaker. My horse
theme enough for them all to talk about. My horse is a fitting subject for a
sovereign to talk about, and for a sovereign's sovereign to ride on; and for the
citizens of the world, whether familiar to us or unknown to us to stop doing
their jobs and wonder at him. I once wrote a sonnet in his praise and began it
in this way: 'Wonder of nature —'"

Orleans interrupted and said, "I have heard a sonnet written to a man's
mistress that began in that way."

The Dauphin said, "Then the writer of that sonnet imitated the sonnet that I composed to my courser, for my horse is my mistress."

Here the Dauphin had used the correct word for a warhorse: a courser.

Orleans said, "Your mistress bears well."

He thought, *That is a good joke. His mistress — the horse — bears his weight well when he rides it. His mistress — a woman — bears his weight well when he rides her.*

The Dauphin said, "You should say, 'bears *me* well.' That is the prescribed praise and perfection of a good and particular mistress. A mistress should be mistress to only one man."

The Constable said, "I thought that yesterday your mistress shrewdly shook your back."

He thought, *That is a good joke. A mistress that shrewdly shakes one's back is not a good mistress. A mistress — a horse — that shrewdly shakes one's back provides a rough ride. A mistress — a woman — that shrewdly shakes one's back may be good in bed but is still a shrew — an evil-tongued woman. Such women can be punished by putting a bridle in their mouth.*

The Dauphin replied, "So perhaps did yours."

"Mine was not bridled."

The Dauphin said, "In that case, she was probably old and gentle; and you rode your mistress like a kern of Ireland — a barefoot Irish peasant pressed into service as a soldier — with your French hose off, and in such tight trousers that you might as well have been barelegged."

The Dauphin thought, *Yes, you would have ridden your mistress while half-stripped for ease of action.*

"You have good judgment in horsemanship," the Constable said.

He thought, *You have good judgment in whoresmanship.*

"Be warned by me," the Dauphin said. "People who ride their mistresses like that and ride without caution fall into foul bogs."

The Dauphin thought, *That is a really dirty joke. If the mistress is a woman, the foul bog is the dirtiest hole in the part of a woman's body that she is least proud of.*

The Dauphin added, "I had rather have my horse as my mistress."

The Constable said, "I prefer to have my mistress be a jade."

A jade could be either a tired old horse or a tired old woman.

The Dauphin replied, "I tell you, Constable, my mistress wears his own hair."

"His own hair" referred to his horse's hair, but listeners could think that the Dauphin had a male human mistress.

The Dauphin thought, *That is a pretty good insult. I am implying that the Constable's mistress — a woman — has lost her hair. Why do women lose their hair? Sometimes it is the result of venereal disease.*

The Constable replied, "I could make as true a boast as that even if I had a sow as my mistress."

The Dauphin replied, "Remember 2 Peter 2:22: '*Le chien est retourne a son propre vomissement, et la truie lavee au bourbier*' ['The dog returns to its own vomit, and the washed sow returns to the mire']. You would make use of anything."

He thought, *That is a major insult. I said that the Constable would make use of anything ... to score a point, but the phrase "make use of" also means "to sleep with."*

The Constable said, "Yet do I not use my horse for my mistress, or any such proverb so little apt to the purpose. Your Biblical quotation has little relevance to the topic of our conversation."

He thought, *That is a pretty good insult: "use [sexually] my horse for my mistress." I am implying that the Dauphin has sex with his horse.*

Rambures wanted to change the topic of conversation; these insults were major.

He asked, "My Lord Constable, the armor that I saw in your tent tonight, are those stars or Suns upon it?"

"Stars, my lord."

The Dauphin said, "Some of them will fall tomorrow, I hope."

The Constable replied, "And yet my sky shall not want. Even if I lose a few stars, I will have plenty more."

The Dauphin said, "That may be, for you bear too many stars, and it would make more honor for you if you were to lose some in battle."

He thought, *That is a major insult. I am telling the Constable that it would be a good thing if his armor showed some signs of having been used.*

The Constable replied, "The stars I bear on my armor are similar to the boasts your horse bears when it bears you on its back. My armor is fine as it is, and your horse would trot just as well if some of your brags dismounted."

The Dauphin replied, "I wish that I could load my horse with all the praises it deserves!"

He added, "Will it never be day? I will trot tomorrow for a mile, and I will pave that mile with English corpses and faces."

The Constable said, "I will not say what you said because if I were you, I would be worried about being faced out of my way — I would be worried about being put to shame and turned from my way. But I wish that it were morning because I would like to be about the ears of the English."

Rambures said, "Will anyone gamble with me for the stake of twenty English prisoners?"

The Constable said, "You must first put yourself in danger in the battle tomorrow, before you have them."

The Dauphin said, "It is midnight; I'll go arm myself."

He departed.

Orleans said, "The Dauphin longs for morning."

Rambures said, "He longs to eat the English."

"I think he will eat all he kills," the Constable said. "In other words, I do not think that he will kill anyone."

"By the white hand of my lady, the Dauphin is a gallant Prince," Orleans said.

"Swear by her foot, so that she can stamp out your oath," the Constable said. "You will find that you will wish that you had not made that oath."

Orleans said, "The Dauphin is absolutely the most active gentleman of France."

The Constable replied, "Doing is activity; and he will always be doing."

He thought, *The Dauphin will always be busy, and always be accomplishing little.*

Orleans still defended the Dauphin, "He never did harm that I heard of."

"He will do no harm to the enemy tomorrow," the Constable said. "He will still keep that good name."

Orleans was persistent: "I know him to be valiant."

The Constable replied, "I was told that by a person who knows him better than you."

"Who told you?"

"He told me so himself; and he said he cared not who knew it."

"He does not need to brag about his valor; it is not a hidden virtue in him."

"I disagree, sir," the Constable said. "No one has ever seen the Dauphin's courage except for his footman: The Dauphin is brave enough to give orders to his footman. The Dauphin's valor is hooded; when the need for his valor appears, it will 'bate."

He thought, *That is a pretty major insult. We keep hawks hooded during the hunt until it is time to release them and let them kill their prey. When the hood is taken off the hawk so that it can hunt, it will bate — spread — its wings. I have said that when the time comes for the Dauphin to show his valor, it will 'bate — that is, it will abate, and shrivel up and die.*

Orleans said, "According to the proverb, ill will never said well. Obviously, you do not like the Dauphin."

The Constable said, "I will top your proverb with this proverb: There is flattery in friendship."

"And I will respond with this proverb: Give the Devil his due."

"Well answered," the Constable said. "Your friend the Dauphin is standing in for the Devil. I respond with this proverb that aims straight at the heart of your proverb: A pox on the Devil."

"You are better than I am at proverbs the way that a fool is better at quickly shooting replies than a wise man is," Orleans said. "Remember this proverb: A fool's bolt, aka blunted arrow, is soon shot. Foolish archers do not wait for the proper time to shoot in battle; they shoot quickly. A wise archer waits for the proper time to shoot."

"You have shot over the target," the Constable said. "Your proverb is not a suitable answer to my proverb — you have missed your target."

"You say that I have shot over the target," Orleans said. "I say that this is not the first time you have overshot — the things that you have said to the Dauphin tonight were way out of line."

A messenger arrived.

The messenger said, "My lord High Constable, the English are camped within fifteen hundred paces of your tents."

"Who has measured the ground?"

"The Lord Grandpré."

"He is a valiant and most expert gentleman," the Constable said. "I wish that it were day! Alas, poor Harry of England! He does not long for the dawn as we do."

Orleans said, "What a wretched and tiresome fellow is this King of England, to blunder aimlessly with his fat-brained, thick-witted followers so much farther from England than he would have gone if he had had even average intelligence!"

"If the English had any intelligence, they would run away," the Constable said.

"They lack intelligence," Orleans said. "Their skulls are so thick that they have no room for brains."

Rambures said, "That island of England breeds very valiant creatures; their mastiffs are of unmatchable courage. We know that from their performance at bear-baiting — they are very competent at tormenting chained bears."

Orleans said, "English mastiffs are foolish curs that run with their eyes closed into the mouth of a Russian bear and have their heads crushed like rotten apples! You may as well say that that's a valiant flea that dares to bite the lip of a lion and drink its breakfast of blood there."

"True," the Constable said, "and the men resemble the mastiffs in robust and rough comings-on, leaving their brains behind with their wives. If you then give them great meals of beef and iron and steel, they will eat like wolves and fight like Devils."

"True," Orleans said, "but these English soldiers are cruelly out of beef."

"Then we will find tomorrow that they have only stomachs to eat and none to fight," the Constable said. "Now it is time to arm. Come, shall we arm?"

Orleans said, "It is now two o'clock, but, let me see, by ten o'clock, we shall each have taken prisoner a hundred Englishmen."

CHAPTER 4

Prologue

The Chorus walked on stage and said, "Now open your minds and imagine a time when creeping murmur and the poring dark fills the wide vessel of the universe. The soldiers talk quietly and strain their eyes trying to see in the dark. The hum of either army quietly sounds, so that the sentinels at their posts almost can hear the secret whispers of each army's watch. Watchfires rise up on both sides, and through their pale flames the soldiers of each army see the other army's soldiers' highlighted yet shadowed faces. Steed threatens steed with high and boastful neighs that pierce the night's dull ear, and from the tents the armorers, fitting the Knights into their armor, busily use hammers to close up the rivets, fastening the helmet to the cuirass. These sounds give dreadful note of preparation for the upcoming battle. The country cocks crow, the clocks toll, and both announce the third hour of drowsy morning.

"Proud of their numbers and sure of forthcoming victory, the confident and arrogant French gamble with dice, using the despised English soldiers they expect to soon take prisoner as their stakes. The French soldiers chide the crippled slow-gaited night that, like a foul and ugly witch, limps so tediously away.

"The poor condemned English, like animals waiting patiently to be sacrificed, by their watchful fires sit patiently and inwardly ruminate about the danger that will come with the morning. Their melancholy bearing, lean cheeks, and war-worn coats make the gazing Moon regard them as so many horrible ghosts.

"Whoever will now behold the royal Captain of this ruined band of English soldiers walking from watch to watch, from tent to tent, let him cry, 'Praise and glory on his head!' For forth King Henry V goes and visits all his soldiers. He bids them good morning with a modest smile and calls them brothers, friends, and countrymen. Upon his royal face there is no sign of how dread an army has surrounded him, nor does he sacrifice even one little bit of color to the weary night throughout which he stays awake. Instead, he looks fresh and suppresses his weariness with a cheerful appearance and sweet majesty.

"Every unhappy soldier, tormented by anxiety and pale in face, who see
him plucks comfort from his looks. His generous eye gives to everyone
universal gift just like the Sun by shining gives a gift to everyone on earth
Harry's looks thaw cold fear, and men of mean origins and men of noble origin
all behold, as my unworthy words declare, a little touch of Harry in the night.

"And so our theatrical scene must to the battle fly, where — it is such
pity! — we shall much disgrace the name of Agincourt by trying to present th
battle on stage with four or five most vile and ragged blunted swords, very evill
wielded in a ridiculous brawl more suited for a tavern than a battlefield.

"Yet sit and see, and imagine what the real battle was like as you watch ou
mere imitation of battle."

— 4.1 —

King Henry V, Bedford, and Gloucester talked together in the Englis
camp.

"Gloucester, it is true that we are in great danger," Henry V said. "Th
greater therefore should our courage be."

He added, "Good morning, brother Bedford.

"God Almighty! There is some quality of goodness hidden even in ev
things, if only men would seek to find it. Here's an example: Our bad neighbor
— the French soldiers — make us early stirrers, which is both healthy an
good time management. In addition, they are our outward consciences, an
preachers to us all, because they admonish us that we should prepare ourselve
fairly for our end and be prepared to die in such a condition that we will g
to Paradise. Thus may we gather nectar and honey from the weed, and learn
moral maxim even from the Devil himself."

Erpingham walked over to the group.

"Good morning, old Sir Thomas Erpingham," Henry V said. "A good sol
pillow for that good white head would be better than a churlish turf of France.

"Not so, my liege," Erpingham replied. "I like this lodging better, becaus
now I can say, 'I live like a King.'"

"It is good for men to have an example of how they can embrace thei
present pains," Henry V said. "It eases and lightens a heavy spirit. When th
mind is quickened, and released from doubt, the bodily organs, although the
were defunct and dead before, end their drowsy sleep and again agilely move

They are like a snake that was sluggish until it sloughed its skin and began to move again with nimbleness and agility.

"Lend me your cloak, Sir Thomas."

Sir Thomas gave his cloak to the King.

"Brothers both, commend me to the Princes in our camp," Henry V said. "Give my greetings to them, and tell them to meet me soon at my tent."

Gloucester replied, "We shall, my liege."

"Shall I go with and attend your grace?" Erpingham asked.

"No, my good Knight," Henry V said. "Go with my brothers to my lords of England. I and my heart must commune for a while, and I want no other company."

Erpingham replied, "The Lord in Heaven bless you, noble Harry!"

Everyone except the King left.

Henry V said to himself, "God bless you, old heart! You speak cheerfully."

Pistol walked over to Henry V, who was disguised by Erpingham's cloak and the darkness.

Pistol asked, "*Qui vous là?*"

This was bad French. Pistol should have asked, "*Qui va là?*" This means, "Who goes there?"

Henry V replied, "A friend."

"Discuss unto me —" Pistol began.

His language was too fancy and not accurate. He should have simply said, "Tell me—"

He continued, "Are you an officer? Or are you of low birth, a common soldier, and an ordinary man?"

"I am a gentleman of a company."

The King's words meant, "I am a person of good birth serving in the King's army."

"Do you trail the puissant pike behind you as you walk?" Pistol asked.

Pikes were wooden spears twelve feet or so in length, and often the soldier would grip a pike behind the spearhead and let the other end of the pike trail — that is, drag — behind him on the ground.

"Yes, I do," Henry V said. "Who are you?"

Pistol replied, "As good a gentleman as the Holy Roman Emperor."

"Then you are higher in rank than the King," Henry V said.

Pistol spoke highly — but overly familiarly — of the King: "The King's a good lad and a heart of gold. He is a lad of life and a lucky and renowned Devil. He comes from good parents, and his fist is most valiant. I kiss his dirty shoe, and from the bottom of my heart I love the lovely young fellow."

As usual, Pistol spoke using over-emphatic language. "I kiss his dirty shoe" meant "I respect him."

Pistol was capable of ordinary, correct language. He asked, "What is your name?"

Henry V replied, "Harry le Roy."

Le roi is French for "the King," so Henry V was telling Pistol the truth.

"Leroy!" Pistol said. "That is a Cornish name. Are you one of the soldiers who came from Cornwell?"

"No, I am a Welshman," Henry V replied.

"Do you know Fluellen?"

"Yes."

"Tell him that I'll knock his leek against his head on Saint Davy's Day."

A leek is an edible vegetable related to the onion. Saint David is the patron saint of Wales, and his annual feast day — Pistol called it "Saint Davy's Day" — is March 1. The leek is Saint David's personal emblem, and many Welch wear a leek on their clothing on Saint David's Day. Fluellen wore a leek in his cap on that day to celebrate his being from Wales.

Henry V replied, "Don't wear your dagger in your cap on that day, or Fluellen will knock your dagger against your head."

"Are you his friend?"

"Yes, and his kinsman, too."

"Here is a middle finger for you, then," Pistol said, making the (in)appropriate gesture.

"I thank you," Henry V said politely. "May God be with you!"

Leaving, Pistol called back over his shoulder, "My name is Pistol."

Alone, King Henry V said to himself, "Your name, Pistol, fits your fierceness."

Captain Fluellen and Captain Gower now approached separately. Unnoticed, Henry V stood quietly in the shadows.

Captain Gower called, "Captain Fluellen!"

Captain Fluellen replied, "In the name of Jesu Christ, speak lower. It is the greatest admiration of the universal world [Everyone is amazed] when the true and aunchient prerogatifes [ancient prerogatives, or rules] and laws of the wars are not kept. If you would take the pains to examine the wars of the ancient Roman general Pompey the Great, you shall find, I promise you, that there is no tiddle toddle [tittle-tattle, aka chattering] nor pibble pabble [bibble-babble, aka babbling] in Pompey's camp. I promise you that you shall find the ceremonies of the wars, and the cares of it, and the forms of it, and the sobriety [seriousness] of it, and the modesty [decency] of it, to be otherwise."

"Why, the enemy is loud," Captain Gower said. "You hear the enemy soldiers all night."

"If the enemy is an ass and a fool and a prating idiot, is it fitting, think you, that we should also, look you, be an ass and a fool and a prating idiot? Do you really believe that?"

Realizing that Captain Fluellen was right, Captain Gower said, "I will speak lower."

Captain Fluellen replied, "I hope that you will."

The two Captains exited, and King Henry V said to himself, "Although it may appear to be a little unconventional and eccentric, there is much care, prudence, and valor in this Welshman."

Three common soldiers — John Bates, Alexander Court, and John Williams now came near the King. The three common soldiers were worried about the nearing battle.

Alexander Court asked, "Friend John Bates, isn't that the morning breaking yonder?"

"I think that it might be," John Bates replied, "but we have no great cause to desire the approach of day."

John Williams said, "We see yonder the beginning of the day, but I think that we shall not stay alive long enough to see the end of this day."

He heard a noise and said, "Who goes there?"

Henry V, still in disguise, said, "A friend."

John Williams asked, "Under which Captain do you serve?"

"Under Sir Thomas Erpingham."

"He is a good old commander and a most kind gentleman," John Williams said. "Please tell us, what does he think of our chances?"

"He thinks that our chances are like those of men shipwrecked on a sandbar who believe that they will be washed off it during the next high tide."

John Bates asked, "Has he said that to the King?"

"No," the disguised Henry V said, "nor is it fitting that he should say that to the King. Although I say this to you in confidence, I think the King is only a man, as I am. The violet smells to him the way it does to me. The sky appears to him the way it does to me. All his senses are only human senses. With his symbols of state laid aside, in his nakedness he appears only as a man, and although his emotions are higher mounted than ours, soaring like a hawk, yet, when they swoop downwards, also like a hawk, they swoop downwards swiftly and far. Therefore, when the King sees reason to fear, as we do, his fears, no doubt, are of the same relish as ours are, and so, reason tells us, no man should appear fearful in front of the King, lest the King, by showing fear, would dishearten his army."

John Bates said, "He may show what outward courage he will, but I believe, even on as cold a night as this is, he would prefer to be in the Thames River in London up to his neck, and I wish that he were there, and me beside him, no matter the consequences, as long as we were finished here. I would rather be in serious trouble in London than be here."

"I will tell you what I truly think about the King," Henry V said. "I truly believe that he would not wish himself anywhere but where he is."

John Bates said, "Then I wish that he were here alone; his life is sure to be ransomed, and many poor men's lives would be saved."

"I dare say that you respect him more than to wish that he were here alone," Henry V said. "I think that you are saying this to find out what other men think. I think that I could not die anywhere so contented as in the King's company, as long as his cause is just and his war is honorable."

"Just? Honorable? That's more than we know," John Williams said.

"Yes," John Bates said, "and it is more than we should seek to know. We know enough, if we know that we are the King's subjects. If his cause is wrong and he is fighting this war for a bad reason, our obedience to the King wipes the crime of it out of us."

"But if the cause is not good, the King himself has a heavy reckoning to make," John Williams said. "On the Judgment Day, all those legs and arms and heads, chopped off in battle, shall join the rest of their body and cry, 'We died such a place. Some of us were swearing, some of us were crying for a surgeon, some were crying because their wives were left impoverished behind them, some were crying because of the debts they owe, some were crying because of their children left behind without a father to provide for them.'

"I am afraid that few die well who die in a battle; for how can they dispose of anything — including their souls — with Christian charity when they are busily engaged in killing? Now, if these men do not die well, it will be a black matter for the King who led them to it; to disobey the King is contrary to every requirement of being the subject of a King. Subjects must obey their King. Isn't it true that whatever a man causes to be done, it is as if that man did that thing himself?"

King Henry V replied, "So, if a son who is sent by his father to do business abroad dies in a state of sin upon the sea, the responsibility for wickedness of the son, according to your reasoning, should be upon the father who sent him abroad. Or if a servant, obeying his master's command to transport a sum of money, is assailed by robbers and dies with many unrepented sins, you would call the business of the master the author of the servant's damnation, but this is not true.

"The King is not bound to take responsibility for the individual endings of his soldiers. The father is not bound to take responsibility for the individual ending of his son. The master is not bound to take responsibility for the individual ending of his servant. Why not? Because they do not intend these deaths when they send these people to do these undertakings.

"Besides, there is no King, no matter how spotless and without fault his cause is, who can use only spotless soldiers when it comes to war. Some soldiers perhaps are guilty of premeditated murder. Some soldiers perhaps are guilty of seducing virgins with broken promises of marriage. Some soldiers perhaps are guilty of going to war in order to escape being held accountable for goring the gentle bosom of peace with pillage and robbery.

"However, even if these men have defeated the law and outrun punishment at home, even though they can outstrip men, they have no wings to fly from God. War is the beadle — the police officer — of God. War is just vengeance — for their previous breach of the King's laws at home, men are punished in the King's war abroad. At home, they were afraid of being hung for their crimes; here, where they thought that they would be safe, they are killed. Therefore, if they die without being spiritually prepared, the King is no more guilty of their damnation than he was guilty of those crimes that they committed back home and for which they are punished here.

"Every subject's duty is the King's, but every subject's soul is his own. Therefore, every soldier in the wars should do what every sick man should do in his bed. He should wash every stain of sin out of his conscience. If he does that and then dies, death will be to him a benefit. If he does not die, the time that he spent washing every stain of sin out of his conscience was blessedly spent in achieving such good preparation for death. If a man does escape dying, it would not be a sin to think that, by making God so generous a gift of his soul, God let him outlive that day to see His greatness and to teach others how they should prepare for death."

John Williams said, "It is certain that when a man dies in a state of sin, the sin is upon his own head — the King is not responsible for it."

John Bates said, "I do not desire that the King should be responsible for me, yet I am determined to fight vigorously for him."

Henry V said, "I myself heard the King say that he would not allow himself to be ransomed."

John Williams was cynical: "Yes, he said so, to make us fight cheerfully, but after our throats are cut, he may be ransomed, and we will be never the wiser."

Henry V said, "If I live to see that happen, I will never trust the King's word afterward."

"Will you punish him for breaking his word?" John Williams asked sarcastically. "All you can do at best is to shoot at the King with a child's toy gun. The King is the King; a poor person with a private grievance against the King is unable to get any satisfaction or revenge. You may as well use a peacock feather to fan the Sun and cool it so much that it turns to ice. You say that you'll never trust the King's word afterward! Admit that it is a foolish thing to say."

"Your reproof of me is definitely too blunt," Henry V said. "I would fight you, if the time were convenient."

"Let it be a quarrel between us, if you live," John Williams said. "We can fight after the battle."

"I welcome your challenge," Henry V said.

"It's dark, so I can't see you very well," John Williams said. "How shall I know you again?"

"Give me something of yours such as a glove that I can attach to my helmet or cap," Henry V said. "After the battle, if you acknowledge that the glove is yours, I will fight you."

"Here's my glove," John Williams said. "Give me one of your gloves."

"Here."

"I will also wear your glove on my helmet or cap," John Williams said. "If you come to me and say, after the battle, 'This is my glove,' then I swear that I will hit you on your head."

"If I live to see your glove, I will challenge you," the King said.

"You may as well make being hanged your goal."

"I will fight you, even if I do it in the King's presence."

"Keep your word," John Williams said. "Fare you well."

"Be friends, you English fools, be friends," John Bates said. "We have lots of French soldiers to fight. You would know that we are greatly outnumbered if you could count."

"Indeed, the French may lay twenty French crowns to one that they will beat us; for they bear their crowns on their shoulders," Henry V said, "but it is no English treason to cut French crowns, and tomorrow the King himself will be a clipper."

Dishonest people used to cut or clip the edges of the coins called crowns. This was a crime because the value of the coin resided in its metal, but as King Henry V had said, to crush the crown — the top of the head — of an enemy in battle was no crime.

The three common soldiers departed, leaving Henry V alone.

The King said to himself, "Upon the King! 'Let us lay our lives, our souls, our debts, our worried wives, our children, and our sins on the King!' We must bear all. Ours is a hard condition; responsibility is born a twin to greatness. Kings must bear much responsibility for the Kingdom. Kings are subject to the critical breath of every fool who is conscious of nothing other than his own problems.

"Kings must do without the infinite heart's-ease that private men — those who are not rulers — enjoy! What do Kings have that private men do not have other than ceremonial display and status? Of what worth are you, you idle ceremony? What kind of god are you, you who suffer more mortal griefs than do your worshippers? What are your rents? What is your income? Oh, ceremony, show me your wealth! What! Is the essence of ceremony merely adoration? Are you anything other than public position, rank, and ritual, things that create awe and fear in other men?

"A King is less happy in being feared than are his subjects who fear him. What does a King often drink instead of sweet homage? The King drinks poisoned flattery.

"Oh, be sick, you great greatness, you great King, and order your ceremony to cure you! Do you think that the fiery fever will go out because adulation blows honorable titles at you? Will the fiery fever dissipate because courtiers kneel and bow low to you? Can you, when you command the beggar to kneel to you, also command the health of the beggar's knee to come to your unhealthy knee? No.

"You proud dream called ceremony, you who play so cunningly with a King's repose, I am a King who exposes and judges you, and I know that the orb, the scepter and the ball, the sword, the mace, the imperial crown, the robe interwoven of gold and pearl, the pompous and long-winded titles that are pronounced before the name of the King, the throne he sits on, nor the tide of pomp that beats upon the high shore of this world — no, not all these, thrice-gorgeous ceremony, not all these, laid in a majestic bed — none of these can sleep as soundly as the wretched slave, who with a filled stomach and a vacant mind goes to bed, crammed with food that he has worked hard to get. He never sees the horrible night, the child of Hell, but, like a footman running beside the Sun-chariot, as soon as the day breaks and light appears in the sky before Sunrise, the wretched slave rises and helps Hyperion, the father of the Sun-god, to his horse, and so he does all through the ever-running years, doing profitable labor, until he reaches his grave.

"Except for ceremony, such a wretch, spending his days in toil and nights in sleep, has a better position than and the advantage over a King. The slave, a member of the country's peace, enjoys that peace, but the unthinking slave little knows what watch the King keeps to maintain the peace — a peace that the peasant is able to enjoy more than the King who works to achieve it for others."

Erpingham walked over to Henry V and said, "My lord, your nobles, who are worried about your absence, go throughout your camp to find you."

"Good old Knight," Henry V said, "bring all of them to my tent. I'll be there before you."

"I shall do it, my lord," Erpingham said and departed.

Alone, King Henry V said, "Oh, God of battles! Steel my soldiers' hearts; do not let them be afraid. Take from them now the ability to count if the numbers of French soldiers opposing them will pluck their courage from them. Today, Lord, do not think about the sin that my father committed when he got possession of the crown! I have had Richard II's body brought to Westminster and honorably interred there, and on his tomb I have bestowed contrite tears greater in number than the drops of blood that fell from his body when he was murdered. Five hundred almsmen I pay to pray twice a day with their withered hands held up to Heaven to pardon Richard II's murder. I have also built two chantries, where the serious and solemn priests sing continually for Richard II's soul. I will do more, although everything that I can do is not enough. More important than the doing of good works is penitence. I am penitent, and I am implore the pardon of God."

Still at a distance from the King but coming closer, Gloucester said, "My liege!"

Henry V said, "My brother Gloucester's voice? Yes. I know your message: You want me to go to my tent. I will go with you. The day, my friends, and all things wait for me."

— 4.2 —

In the French camp, the Dauphin, Orleans, Rambures, and other soldiers were preparing for the battle.

Orleans shouted, "The Sun is making our armor shine. Mount up, my lords!"

The Dauphin shouted, "*Montez à cheval*! [Mount your horses!] My horse! Varlet! Bring me my horse!"

Orleans said, "Oh, brave spirit!"

The Dauphin said, "*Via! Les eaux et la terre!* [We will go across water and land!]"

Orleans responded, "*Rien puis l'air et la feu*? [And not across air and fire?]"

"*Ciel* [The Heavens], kinsman Orleans," the Dauphin said.

He saw the Constable arriving and called, "Is it time now, my Lord Constable?"

The Constable replied, "Listen at how our steeds neigh! They are ready to go immediately to the battle."

"Mount them," the Dauphin said, "and dig your spurs into their sides so that their blood will spurt into English eyes, and blind them with the horse's excessive red blood, the sign of courage."

"What, will you have the English soldiers weep our horses' blood?" Rambures asked. "How shall we, then, behold their natural tears?"

A messenger arrived and said, "The English are in formation for battle, you French peers."

"To horse, you gallant Princes!" the Constable shouted, rallying his troops. "Immediately mount your horses! If you only look at yonder poor and starved band of English soldiers, your fair show shall suck away their souls, leaving them only the shells and husks of men. There is not work enough for all our soldiers; there is scarcely enough blood in all their sickly veins to give each of our unsheathed swords a stain. Many of our French gallants shall today draw out their swords and then sheathe them again because of a lack of English soldiers to kill. Let us but blow on the English soldiers, and the vapor of our valor will send them sprawling.

"Doubtless, lords, our superfluous servants and our peasants, who unnecessarily swarm around our square battle formations, are enough to purge this field of such a contemptible foe, though we upon this nearby mountain's foot stood inactively looking on, but our honor will not allow us to be mere onlookers.

"What's left to say? Let each of us do a very little, and all will be done. So let the trumpets sound the note to mount and to march. Our approach shall so much dismay the English soldiers that they shall crouch down in fear and surrender. We will be like hunting hawks that fly overhead and make the birds that are prey quiver so fearfully that they may be easily captured."

Grandpré arrived and said, "Why do you stay so long, my lords of France? Yonder corpses-to-be from the British island, who have no hope of saving their bones, ill befit — and disgrace — the battlefield this morning. Their ragged banners, hanging in the air, make a poor show. Our air shakes them very scornfully. Big Mars — the King of England — looks like a bankrupt in his beggarly army and faintheartedly peeps through his helmet's rusty faceguard. The English horsemen sit like fixed candlesticks with torches in their hands — they look like inanimate objects, not like men of spirit. Their poor jades hang their heads and lower their hides and hips, with the gummy discharge from ieir as-pale-as-if-they-were-dead eyes hanging down in long strings. In each de's pale dull mouth, the jointed bit is dirty with chewed grass, completely iotionless. And the knavish crows — the executors who will claim the corpses f the English soldiers and horses after the battle — fly over them, all impatient ir their hour. Description cannot clothe itself in words in such a way to dequately describe the life of such an army that is so lacking in life."

The Constable said, "They have said their prayers, and they are waiting to ie."

The Dauphin asked, sarcastically, "Shall we go send them dinners and fresh its of clothing and give their fasting horses provender, and only afterward ght with them? That might make it more of a fair fight."

The Constable said, "I am waiting for my pennant, but let's go to the attlefield. To save time, I will take the banner from a trumpet and use it as iy pennant. Come, come, let's go! The Sun is high, and we are wasting the aylight."

— 4.3 —

In the English camp were standing Gloucester, Bedford, Exeter, rpingham, Salisbury, and Westmoreland, among others.

Gloucester asked, "Where is the King?"

Bedford replied, "The King himself has ridden to view the French army's attle formation."

"The French have sixty thousand fighting men," Westmoreland said.

"They outnumber us five to one," Exeter said. "In addition, the French oops are all fresh."

"May God's arm strike with us!" Salisbury said. "Those are fearful odds. iod be with you, Princes. I am going to my troops. If we meet no more until we ieet in Heaven, then we will meet joyfully. My noble Lord of Bedford, my dear ord Gloucester, and my good Lord Exeter, and my kind kinsmen, warriors all, dieu!"

"Farewell, good Salisbury," Bedford said, "and may good luck go with you!"

"Farewell, kind lord," Exeter said. "Fight valiantly today, and yet I do you rong to tell you that because you are made of the firm truth of valor."

Salisbury departed.

Bedford said, "He is as full of valor as of kindness; he is Princely in both."

King Henry V arrived, but many people were present and he was no immediately noticed.

The date was 25 October 1415, and it was a feast day in England. O 25 October 286, two twin brothers who were later named saints, Crispin an Crispinian, were martyred.

Westmoreland said, "I wish that we now had here just ten thousand c those men in England who do no work today!"

Henry V asked, "Who is he who wishes that? My kinsman Westmoreland No, my fair kinsman. If we are marked to die, we are enough to do our countr loss; and if we are marked to live, the fewer the men fighting in this battle, th greater share of honor each man of us will have.

"By God's will, I hope that you will not wish for even one man more. B Jove, I am not covetous for gold, nor do I care who eats at my expense, and does not grieve me if other men wear my clothing — such material things d not dwell among my desires. But if it is a sin to covet honor, I am the mo offending soul alive.

"No, by my faith, my kinsman, do not wish that even a single man fror England could be added to our army here. By God's peace, I would not lose a much honor as one man more, I think, would take from me for the best hop I have — the hope for my salvation. That is how covetous I am for honor an glory. Oh, do not wish for even one man more!

"Instead, proclaim, Westmoreland, throughout my army, that he who ha no stomach for this fight is permitted to depart. He shall be given a letter t allow him passage through foreign lands, and crowns to pay for his journe shall be put into his purse. We do not want to die in the company of a man wh fears to die with us in brotherhood.

"This day is the feast day of Saint Crispinian. Any soldier who outlives thi day, and returns safely home to our island, will proudly stand tall when this da is named, and raise himself up at the name of Crispinian.

"He who shall outlive this day, and see his old age, will yearly on the eve c this day feast his neighbors and say, 'Tomorrow is Saint Crispinian's feast day Then will he roll up his sleeves and show his scars and say, 'These wounds earned on Saint Crispinian's feast day.'

"Old men forget, yet when everything else shall be forgotten, he' remember — with embellishments — what feats he did on this day. At tha time our names, as familiar in his mouth as household words — Harry the King, Bedford and Exeter, Warwick and Talbot, Salisbury and Gloucester — shall be freshly remembered as men drink their flowing cups.

"This story shall the good man teach his son, and the feast day of Saint Crispin and Saint Crispinian shall never go by, from this day through the ending of the world, without us being remembered — we few, we happy few, we band of brothers.

"For he today who sheds his blood with me shall be my brother. No matter how lowly he was born, this day shall raise his status. Gentlemen in England who are now in bed shall think themselves cursed because they were not here, and they will be ashamed and think that they lack courage as they listen to anyone who fought with us upon Saint Crispin and Saint Crispinian's day."

Salisbury arrived and said, "My sovereign lord, quickly prepare yourself for the battle. The French are splendidly set in their battle formations, and they will soon with all convenient speed charge on us."

Henry V said, "All things are ready, if our minds are ready."

Westmoreland said, "Perish the man whose mind is backward now!"

Henry V asked, "You do not wish for more help from England, kinsman?"

"No, by God!" Westmoreland said. "My liege, I wish that you and I alone, without help, could fight this royal battle!"

"Why, now you have wished that we had five thousand fewer men," Henry V said. "I prefer that to your wishing that we had one more man."

He said to everyone present, "You know your places: God be with you all!"

A trumpet sounded to announce the arrival of Montjoy, the French envoy, who said, "Once more I come to learn from you, King Harry, whether you will make a bargain for your ransom before this battle that you will certainly lose. Right now, you are so near the abyss of danger that danger will swallow you. In addition, because he is merciful, the Constable asks you to remind your soldiers to repent their sins so that when they die today their souls will make a peaceful and sweet journey away from this battlefield where, poor wretches, their bodies will lie and fester."

"Who has sent you now?" Henry V asked.

"The Constable of France."

"Please, take back to him the same answer that I previously gave to you. Tell the French soldiers to defeat and take me and then sell my bones.

"Good God! Why should they mock poor fellows thus? A man once sold the skin of a lion while the beast still lived — that man was killed while hunting the lion.

"Many of our bodies shall no doubt find native graves back home on our native islands. This day's work shall be witnessed in the brass funeral monuments that will mark their graves.

"Others will leave their valiant bones in France. They will die like men, though they will be buried in your dunghills. They shall be famed; for even there the Sun shall greet them, and draw their honors like steam up to Heaven, leaving their earthly reeking, decomposing bodies behind to choke your environment: The smell of their corpses shall breed a plague in France.

"You will see then the abundant valor in our English soldiers, who despite being dead, are similar to a cannonball's breaking into pieces and causing a second course of death and destruction, despite its own destruction.

"Let me speak proudly. Tell the constable that we are only warriors for the working day; we look like we are wearing workingmen's clothing. Our fancy and gilded clothing is all muddy because we have marched through rain to finally get to this battlefield. There's not a piece of feather to serve as a helmet-plume in our army — a sign, I hope, that no one will fly away from the battle — and time has worn us into scruffiness.

"But, by the Mass, our hearts are still trim and in perfect condition, and my poor soldiers tell me that before this night comes that either they will be wearing fresher robes in Paradise or they will pluck the gay new coats over the French soldiers' heads and dismiss them from military service.

"If they do this — as, if God is willing, they shall — whatever ransom I ask from you will easily be collected because we will seize your French treasure. Herald, save your labor. Do not come here any more to ask me for a ransom, gentle herald.

"You French shall receive no ransom, I swear, but these my joints. I intend to die before I allow you to take them, and therefore this ransom will yield you little value. Tell the Constable that."

Montjoy replied, "I shall, King Harry. And so fare you well. You shall never hear from me any more."

As Montjoy exited, Henry V called after him, "I'm afraid that you will return to ask me what ransom I demand from you French."

York came over to Henry V, knelt, and said, "My lord, most humbly on my knee I beg you to allow me to command the vanguard — the troops at the front."

Henry V replied, "Take their command, brave York. Now, soldiers, march away, and to whomever You wish, God, give the victory!"

— 4.4 —

On the battlefield, Pistol was ferociously taking a frightened French soldier prisoner. The Boy was with them.

Pistol shouted, "Surrender, you dog!"

The French soldier replied, "*Je pense que vous etes gentilhomme de bonne qualite.* [I think you are a gentleman of good quality and high rank.]"

Pistol replied, "*Qualtitie calmie custure me*!"

Pistol, who was poor in French, wanted to know the French soldier's quality, aka social class. If the French soldier were highborn, then Pistol would be able to get a high ransom for him. Pistol had meant to say, "*Quel titre comme accoster me*!" This is French, more or less, for, "What title as accost me?" It asks, more or less, what Pistol was most interested in learning the answer to; of course, Pistol being Pistol, he mispronounced the words, of which he had little understanding.

He added in English, "Are you a gentleman? What is your name? Discuss."

"*Seigneur Dieu*! [Lord God!]" the French soldier replied.

Thinking that the French soldiers had stated his name, Pistol said, "Signieur Dew must be a gentleman. Perpend my words, Signieur Dew, and note them: Signieur Dew, you will die at the end of my sword, unless, Signieur, you give to me egregious ransom."

As usual, Pistol was using extravagant language.

"*Prenez misericorde*! *Ayez pitie de moi*! [Have mercy! Take pity on me!]" the French soldier said.

Hearing *moi* and thinking that it was perhaps a French coin or a French version of the word "moiety," which means a lesser share, or sometimes half, Pistol said, "*Moy* shall not serve. I will have forty *moys*, or I will reach down your throat, grab your insides, and pull them out through your throat along with drops of crimson blood."

"*Est-il impossible d'echapper la force de ton bras*? [Is it impossible to escape the force of your arm?]" the French soldier said.

85

Hearing *bras*, French for arm, and thinking that it meant a brass coin, Pistol said, "Brass, you dog! You damned and overly sexed mountain goat, are you offering to give me brass coins as a ransom?"

"*Pardonnez moi*! [Forgive me!]"

"What are you saying?" Pistol asked. "A tun [barrel] of moys?"

He then said to the Boy, "Come here, Boy. Ask this slave in French what his name is."

The Boy said, "*Ecoutez: comment etes-vous appele*? [Listen to me: What is your name?]."

"*Monsieur le Fer.*"

Fer is French for "iron."

The Boy said, "He says his name is Master Fer."

"Master Fer!" Pistol said. "I'll fer him, and firk [beat] him, and ferret [torment] him. Discuss the same in French to him."

"I do not know the French for 'fer,' and 'ferret,' and 'firk.'"

Pistol replied, "Tell him to prepare to die because I will cut his throat."

The French soldier asked the Boy, "*Que dit-il, monsieur*? [What is he saying, Master?"]

The Boy replied, "*Il me commande de vous dire que vous faites vous pret; car ce soldat ici est dispose tout a cette heure de couper votre gorge.* [He is ordering me to tell you to prepare to die because he intends to cut your throat right now.]"

Pistol said, "*Owy, cuppele gorge, permafoy.*"

Owy is Pistol's bad French for *oui*, or "yes." *Cuppele gorge* is Pistol's bad French for *couper la gorge*, or "cut the throat." *Permafoy* is Pistol's French for *per ma foi*, or "on my faith."

Pistol added, "Peasant, unless you give me crowns, brave crowns, I will mangle you with my sword."

The French soldier said, "*Je vous supplie, pour l'amour de Dieu, me pardonner! Je suis gentilhomme de bonne maison: gardez ma vie, et je vous donnerai deux cents ecus.* [I beg you, for the love of God, pardon me! I am a gentleman of good family: Save my life, and I will give you two hundred crowns.]"

Pistol asked the Boy, "What are his words?"

"He begs you to save his life. He says that he is a gentleman of a good house, and for his ransom he will give you two hundred crowns."

"Tell him my fury shall abate, and I his crowns will take."

"*Petit monsieur, que dit-il*? [Little man, what did he say?]" the French soldier asked.

The Boy replied, "*Encore qu'il est contre son jurement de pardoner aucun prisonnier, neanmoins, pour les ecus que vous l'avez promis, il est content de vous donner la liberte, le franchisement.* [Although it is against his oath not to pardon any prisoners, he is nevertheless willing to accept the crowns you have offered him and to give you your liberty, your freedom.]"

The French soldier said, "*Sur mes genoux je vous donne mille remercimens; je m'estime heureux que je suis tombe entre les mains d'un chevalier, je pense, le plus brave, vaillant, et tres distingue seigneur d'Angleterre.* [On my knees, I thank you a thousand times, and I consider myself fortunate to have been captured by a gentleman whom I believe is the bravest, most valiant, and most distinguished nobleman of England.]"

"Expound what he said to me, boy," Pistol ordered.

"He gives you, upon his knees, a thousand thanks," the Boy said, "and he esteems himself happy that he has fallen into the hands of a man who he thinks is the bravest, most valorous, and worthiest Signieur of England."

"As I suck blood, I will show some mercy to him," Pistol said.

Pistol spoke truly. He had come to France to suck blood like a leech. He had come to France to make money, not to gain honor.

Pistol said to his prisoner, "Follow me!"

The Boy said to the prisoner, "*Suivez-vous le grand capitaine.* [Follow the great Captain.]"

Pistol and his prisoner departed, leaving the Boy alone, who said to himself, I have never known so loud a voice to come from so empty a heart — Pistol is a coward. But this saying is true: 'The empty vessel makes the greatest sound.' Bardolph and Nym had ten times more courage than Pistol, who is like the roaring Devil in the old morality plays. The Devil roars, and yet in the plays everyone is able to cut his fingernails with a wooden dagger. Although Bardolph and Nym had ten times more courage than Pistol, they are both hanged. Pistol would also be hanged if he dared to steal anything with any kind of spirit at all — he is the pettiest of petty thieves.

"I must stay with the other servants with the baggage in our camp. The French soldiers would have an easy time attacking the camp if they were to do it because there is no one to guard the camp except us boys."

— 4.5 —

In another part of the battlefield, the Constable, Orleans, Bourbon, the Dauphin, and Rambures were shocked by how well the English army was fighting. Despite being heavily outnumbered, the English army was routing the French army.

The Constable said, "*Oh, Diable*! [Oh, Hell!]"

Orleans said, "*Oh, Seigneur! Le jour est perdu, tout est perdu!* [Oh, Lord God! The day is lost — everything is lost!]"

The Dauphin said, "*Mort de ma vie*! [Death of my life!] All is confounded, all! Reproach and everlasting shame sit mocking in the plumes of our helmets. *Oh, merchante fortune*! [Oh, evil fortune!]"

He added, "Do not run away."

The Constable said, "Why, all our ranks are broken."

"Oh, everlasting shame," the Dauphin said. "Let's stab and kill ourselves. Can these be the wretches that we used as stakes when we gambled with dice?"

"Is this the King we sent a herald to, to ask about his ransom?" Orleans said.

"Shame and eternal shame, nothing but shame!" Bourbon said. "Let us die with honor. Let us go back to fight once more. And anyone who will not follow Bourbon and fight now, let him go from here, and with his cap in his hand, like a base panderer, let him stand by the bedroom door while his most beautiful daughter is raped by a slave who has no better ancestors than my dog!"

"Disorder, which has ruined us, be our friend now!" the Constable said. "We were disorganized and so we lost the battle. Now let us go into the disorder of the battle among the heaps of dead and lose our own lives."

"We have enough soldiers yet living in the battlefield that we could smother and defeat the English soldiers with our throngs of men," Orleans said, "if we could bring any order to our troops."

"The Devil take order now!" Bourbon said. "I'll go to the throng of men, fight, and die. Let my life be short, or else shame will live too long."

They returned to the battle.

— 4.6 —

In another part of the battlefield, King Henry V, Exeter, some English soldiers, and others were meeting. They knew that the battle was going well, but they did not know how well. Exeter had news to give to the King.

Henry V said, "We have fought well, most valiant countrymen, but we are not yet done fighting. The French army is still on the battlefield."

Exeter said, "The Duke of York commends him to your majesty."

"Is he still alive, good uncle?" Henry V asked. "Three times within this hour I saw him down; three times I saw him rise up again and fight, although he was bloody from his helmet to his spurs."

Exeter replied, "And in such bloody garb just as you described him, that brave soldier lies and enriches the ground with his blood, and by his bloody side, with similar wounds that give him honor, the noble Earl of Suffolk also lies. Suffolk died first, and York, hacked all over, went to him, where he lay soaked in blood and lifted his head and kissed the bloody gashes that opened wide in his face, and cried aloud, 'Wait, dear kinsman Suffolk! My soul shall keep your soul company as we journey to Heaven. Wait, sweet soul, for my soul, and then we can fly to Heaven side by side just as in this glorious and well-fought battle we kept together as brother-Knights!'

"Hearing these words, I went to him and comforted him. He smiled at me, reached his hand out to me, and, with a feeble grip, said, 'My dear lord, commend my service to my sovereign.'

"He then turned and over Suffolk's neck he threw his wounded arm and kissed Suffolk's lips, and knowing that he was married to death, with his red blood he sealed a final testament of noble-ending love. His final act as he died a noble death was to confirm the love he had for Suffolk.

"The noble and sweet manner of his final act forced those waters from me that I would have stopped — I cried. I had not so much of man and stoical masculinity in me as would have stopped those tears. Instead, all the emotions I inherited from my mother welled up in my eyes and tears trickled down my cheeks."

"I don't blame you for crying," Henry V said, "because, hearing your story, I am forced to wipe my eyes, or tears will also trickle down my cheeks."

War trumpets sounded.

Hearing them, King Henry V said, "What new call to arms is this? The French have reinforced and organized their scattered men. I now give the order for every English soldier to kill his French prisoners. Communicate this order to my soldiers."

King Henry V was afraid that he did not have enough soldiers both to fight the French army and to guard the French prisoners. He believed that it was necessary to kill the French prisoners so that more English soldiers would be available to fight the French army.

— 4.7 —

As the Boy had said, the French soldiers were able to easily raid the English camp because only boys were guarding it. However, the French soldiers had done more than loot the belongings of the English soldiers; they had killed the boys who were supposed to be guarding it. The Boy was now dead.

Captain Fluellen said to Captain Gower, "Kill the poys [boys] and the luggage! It is expressly against the law of arms [code of military conduct]. It is as arrant [complete] a piece of knavery, mark you now, as can be offered. In your conscience, now, don't you agree?"

Captain Gower replied, "It is certain there's not a boy left alive, and the cowardly rascals who ran from the battle have done this slaughter; in addition, they have burned and carried away all that was in the King's tent. For this reason, the King, most deservedly, has caused every soldier to cut his prisoner's throat. Henry V is a gallant King!"

Captain Gower was wrong about Henry V's reason for cutting the French prisoners' throats.

Captain Fluellen said, "Ay, Henry V was porn [born] at Monmouth, Captain Gower. What call you the town's name where Alexander the Pig [Big] was born!"

You mean Alexander the Great," Captain Gower replied.

"Why, let me ask you, is not pig [big] the same thing as great?" Fluellen said, "The pig [big], or the great, or the mighty, or the huge, or the magnanimous, are all one reckonings [all the same thing], except the phrase is a little variations [except the wording is a little different]."

Captain Gower said, "I think Alexander the Great was born in the country of Macedon; his father was called Philip of Macedon, as I remember it."

Fluellen agreed: "I think it is in Macedon where Alexander is porn [born]. I tell you, Captain, if you look in the maps of the world, I warrant you shall find, in the comparisons between Macedon and Monmouth, that the situations,

90

look you, is both alike. There is a river in Macedon, and there is also moreover a river at Monmouth: It is called Wye at Monmouth; but it is out of my prains [brains; it is out of my brains = I can't remember] what is the name of the other river; but it is all one — the two rivers are as alike as my fingers are to my fingers, and there is salmon in both rivers.

"If you look at Alexander's life well, Harry of Monmouth's life follows it very closely; for there are comparisons and parallels in all things.

"Alexander, God knows, and you know, in his rages, and his furies, and his wraths, and his cholers, and his moods, and his displeasures, and his indignations, and also being a little intoxicated in his prains [brains], did, in his ales and his angers [while intoxicated and angry], look you, kill his best friend, Cleitus."

"Our King is not like him in that," Captain Gower said. "He never killed any of his friends."

Bardolph was dead, hung after disobeying one of Henry V's orders, but Captain Gower did not regard Bardolph as the King's friend.

Fluellen replied, "It is not well done, look you, now to take the tale out of my mouth before it is made and finished. I speak only about the figures and comparisons of it: Just as Alexander killed his friend Cleitus, being in his ales and his cups; so also Harry Monmouth, being in his right wits and his good judgments, turned away the fat Knight with the great belly-doublet — his belly stuffed his jacket. His fat friend was full of jests, and gipes [gibes], and knaveries, and mocks; I have forgotten his name."

"Sir John Falstaff," Captain Gower said.

"That is he," Captain Fluellen said. "I'll tell you there is good men porn [born] at Monmouth."

"Here comes his majesty," Captain Gower said.

King Henry V and several soldiers arrived, along with Warwick, Gloucester, Exeter, and others.

Henry V, who had just heard about the boys at the English camp being murdered, said, "I was not angry since I came to France until I became angry at this instant. Take a trumpet, herald, and ride to the French horsemen on yonder hill. If they are willing to fight with us, tell them to come down from the hill and fight. If they are not willing to fight, tell them to leave the battlefield because they offend our sight.

"If they'll neither fight nor leave, we will come to them, and make them scurry away as swiftly as the stones forcibly thrown from the ancient Assyrians' slings. In addition, we will cut the throats of these new prisoners we have taken, and not a man of them whom we shall defeat shall taste our mercy. Go and tell them so."

An English herald exited.

Montjoy, the main French herald, entered.

Exeter said, "Here comes the herald of the French, my liege."

Gloucester observed, "His eyes are humbler than they used to be."

"Well!" Henry V said. "What do you want, herald? You already know that I named as my ransom these bones of mine. Have you come to me again to ask me to ransom myself?"

"No, great King," Montjoy said. "I come to you for charitable and Christian permission for we French to wander over this bloody battlefield to look for our dead, and then to bury them. We want to sort our nobles from our common men because many of our Princes — so many! — lie drowned and soaked in the blood of soldiers we paid to fight for us. Our common soldiers drench their peasant limbs with the blood of Princes; and their wounded steeds fret fetlock deep in gore and with wild rage kick out their armed heels at their dead masters, killing them twice. Oh, give us leave, great King, to view the field in safety and dispose of our soldiers' dead bodies!"

Henry V said, "I tell you truly, herald, that I do not know whether we have won the battle or not because many of your horsemen still gallop over the battlefield."

"The day is yours," Montjoy said. "You have won the battle."

"Praised be God, and not our strength, for it!" Henry V said. "What is the name of this castle that stands nearby?"

"They call it Agincourt," Montjoy replied.

"Then we call this the battlefield of Agincourt," Henry V said. "We have fought and won the Battle of Agincourt on the feast day of Saint Crispin and Saint Crispinian."

Captain Fluellen said to the King, "Your great-grandfather of famous memory, if it please your majesty, and your great-uncle Edward the Plack [Black] Prince of Wales, as I have read in the chronicles, fought a most prave pattle [brave battle] here in France."

"They did, Fluellen."

"Your majesty says very truly," Fluellen said. "If your majesty is remembered of it, the Welshmen did good service in a garden where leeks did grow, wearing leeks in their knitted round caps from Monmouth, Wales — leeks, your majesty knows, to this hour are an honorable badge of the service because they are worn by many soldiers, and I do believe your majesty takes no scorn to wear the leek upon Saint Tavy's [Davy's, aka David's] day."

Henry V thought, *"… did good service in a garden where leeks did grow" sounds like the Welshmen ate a lot in the garden, but Fluellen means that the Welshmen did good military service.*

Henry V said, "I wear the leek for a memorable honor because I am Welsh, you know, good countryman."

"All the water in Wye River cannot wash your majesty's Welsh plood [blood] out of your pody [body], I can tell you that: God pless [bless] it and preserve it, as long as it pleases His grace, and his majesty, too!"

"Thanks, my good countryman."

"By Jeshu [Jesus], I am your majesty's countryman," Fluellen said. "I care not who knows it; I will confess it to all the world: I need not be ashamed of your majesty, praised be God, as long as your majesty is an honest man."

"May God keep me honest!" Henry V said.

John Williams walked up to the group. He was one of the common soldiers whom Henry V, while incognito, had talked to before the battle. John Williams had criticized him, and the two had exchanged tokens — gloves. The two men were supposed to attach the gloves to their caps after the battle, if they survived. If either man were to recognize his glove, the two men had pledged to fight each other. John Williams had attached the King's glove to his cap. But Henry V had not attached John Williams' glove to his cap.

King Henry V ordered some of his men, "Our heralds will now go with Montjoy. Bring me accurate numbers of the dead of both armies."

The English heralds and Montjoy departed.

Henry V noticed John Williams, pointed to him, and said, "Call yonder man here."

Exeter said to John Williams, "Soldier, you must come to the King."

When John Williams had come closer, Henry asked him, "Soldier, why are you wearing that glove in your cap?"

"If it please your majesty, it is the gage of one whom I will fight, if he is still alive now that the battle has ended. I am wearing his glove, and if he dares to acknowledge that it is his, then he and I will fight."

"An Englishman?" the King asked.

"If it please your majesty, he is a rascal who swaggered and blustered and quarreled with me last night; and if he is alive and dares to acknowledge that this glove is his, I have sworn to hit him on the ear. Or if I can see my glove in his cap, which he swore, as he was a soldier, he would wear if he were still alive after the battle, I will knock it off."

"What do you think, Captain Fluellen?" Henry V asked. "Is it fitting that this soldier keep his oath?"

"He is a craven coward and a villain else, if it please your majesty, according to my conscience," Fluellen replied.

"Perhaps his enemy is a high-ranking gentleman who because of his status cannot fight a common soldier," Henry V said.

"Though he be as good a gentleman as the Devil is — and the Devil is thought to be in some sense a gentleman — as good a gentleman as Lucifer and Beelzebub himself, it is necessary, look your grace, that he keep his vow and his oath," Captain Fluellen said. "If he perjures himself, see you now, his reputation is as arrant a villain and a Jack Sauce [saucy Jack, or saucy fellow, aka rascal and saucebox], as ever his black shoe trod upon God's ground and his earth, in my conscience."

The King told John Williams, "Then keep your vow, young man, when you meet the man whose glove you are wearing."

"So I will, my liege," John Williams said. "I am alive, I survived the battle, and I will keep my promise to fight him."

"Under whom do you serve?" Henry V asked.

"Under Captain Gower, my liege."

"Captain Gower is a good Captain, and he has a good knowledge of and is well read in military history," Captain Fluellen said.

Henry V said to John Williams, "Go to him and tell him to come to me, soldier."

"I will, my liege."

He departed.

King Henry V then said, "Here, Fluellen; wear this token — this glove — for me. Attach it to your cap."

Henry V handed him John Williams' glove.

He then added, "When the Duke of Alençon and I were fighting, I plucked this glove from his helmet. If any man recognizes this glove and wants to fight you, he is a friend to the Duke of Alençon and he is an enemy to our person. If you encounter any such person, arrest him, if you support me."

"Your grace does me as great honors as can be desired in the hearts of his subjects," Fluellen said. "I would like to see any man with two legs who shall think himself aggrieved by this glove — that is all I can say. I would like to see it once, if it please God of His grace that I might see him."

"Do you know Captain Gower?" Henry V asked.

"He is my dear friend, if it please you," Fluellen said.

"Please, go and find him, and bring him to my tent," Henry V said.

"I will fetch him."

Fluellen departed to find Captain Gower.

Henry V then said, "My Lord of Warwick, and my brother Gloucester, follow Fluellen closely at his heels. The glove that I have just given him may perhaps get him a blow on his ear. This glove belongs to the soldier John Williams. According to the agreement I made with him, I should wear it myself, but I want to play a joke. I have arranged it so that Fluellen and John Williams will meet at my tent.

"Follow Fluellen, good kinsman Warwick. If the soldier John Williams strikes him, as I judge by his blunt bearing he will keep his word to do so, some sudden harm — bloodshed — may arise from it because I know that Fluellen is valiant, and when he is touched by anger the way that a cannon is touched by a match that fires it, then he is as hot as gunpowder, and he will quickly pay back an insult. Follow Fluellen and see that no harm comes to him and the common soldier."

He then said, "Come with me, uncle of Exeter. Let's go to my tent and witness the fun."

— 4.8 —

Captain Gower and John Williams were speaking in front of the tent of the King.

95

John Williams said to Captain Gower, "I think that the King wants to see you in order to make you a Knight."

In search of Captain Gower, Captain Fluellen, who also believed that the King was going to Knight Captain Gower, arrived and said to him, "By God's will and His pleasure, Captain, I ask you now to come quickly to the King; there is more good coming to you perhaps than is in your knowledge to dream of."

John Williams saw the glove displayed on Captain Fluellen's hat and recognized that it was his glove. He understandably assumed that Captain Fluellen was the man with whom he had quarreled the previous night. He held up the glove that the King had given to him the previous night and said to Captain Fluellen, "Sir, do you recognize this glove?"

"Recognize the glove!" Fluellen said. "I recognize that the glove is a glove."

"I recognize the glove that you are wearing in your cap," John Williams said. "I accept your challenge to fight."

He then hit the glove, which was over Fluellen's ear. In doing so, he also hit Fluellen.

"By God's blood!" Fluellen cursed. "You are as arrant a traitor as any traitor in the universal world, or in France, or in England!"

Captain Gower was shocked that one of the soldiers serving under him would hit a Captain. He said to John Williams, "What are you doing? Sir, you are a villain!"

John Williams said to Captain Fluellen, "Did you think that I would break my oath to fight you if I saw you with my glove?"

Fluellen said, "Stand back, Captain Gower; I will give this traitor his deserved payment in plows [blows], I promise you."

John Williams replied, "I am no traitor."

"That's a lie in your throat," Captain Fluellen said. He told the soldiers who had gathered around, "I charge you in his majesty's name, apprehend him: He's a friend of the French Duke Alençon's."

Warwick and Gloucester now entered the scene.

"What is going on?" Warwick said. "What's the matter?"

Captain Fluellen replied, "My Lord of Warwick, here is — praised be God for it! — a most contagious and pestilential treason come to light, look you, as you shall desire to see in a summer's day."

He looked up and saw King Henry V approaching and added, "Here is his majesty."

Henry V and Exeter approached the group of men.

Henry V asked, "What's the matter?"

Captain Fluellen replied, "My liege, here is a villain and a traitor, that, look your grace, has struck the glove that your majesty took off of the helmet of the Duke of Alençon."

John Williams said, "My liege, this is my glove; here is the other one; and he to whom I gave it in exchange for a glove of his promised to wear it on his cap, and I promised to strike him, if he did. I just now met this man with my glove on his cap, and I have been as good as my word."

"Your majesty hear now, saving your majesty's manhood, what an arrant, rascally, beggarly, lousy knave this man is," Captain Fluellen said. "I hope your majesty will appear on my behalf and give testimony and witness, and will give avouchment, that this is the glove of Alençon, that your majesty is give me, in your conscience, now."

"Give me your glove, the one you are wearing on your cap, soldier," Henry V said to John Williams. "Look, here is the fellow of it. These are my gloves. It was I, indeed, whom you promised to strike, and you criticized me with the most bitter terms."

Captain Fluellen said, "If it please your majesty, let his neck answer for it — hang him — if there is any martial law in the world."

John Williams was surprised and dismayed. The King could easily give the order to have him hanged, and if the King did give the order, that order would be quickly obeyed. Striking the King — or threatening to strike the King — was definitely cause enough for hanging.

The King asked him, "How can you make things right with me?"

"All offences, my lord, come from the heart," John Williams said. "Never has anything come from my heart that might offend your majesty."

"It was ourself you did abuse with language," the King said.

"Your majesty came not like yourself," John Williams, now kneeling, said. "You did not look like the King. You appeared to me only as a common man such as myself. Remember that it was night, and that you wore a worn cloak, and you appeared to be a lowly, common soldier. Whatever words your highness suffered while you were in disguise, I beg you take it for your own fault and not mine because if you had been the common soldier whom I took you for, I would have committed no offence; therefore, I beg your highness to pardon me."

The King gave a glove to Exeter and said, "Here, uncle Exeter, fill this glove with gold coins, and give it to this man."

He then said to John Williams, who stood up, "Keep this glove, soldier; and wear it in your cap to show others that you have challenged the King himself."

He joked, "Wear this glove on your cap until I answer the challenge."

He said to Exeter, "Give him the crowns."

Finally, he said to Captain Fluellen, "Captain, you must become friends with this soldier."

Captain Fluellen said, "By this day and this light, the fellow has mettle and courage enough in his belly. Wait, here is twelve pence more for you; and I pray you to serve Got [God], and keep yourself out of prawls [brawls], and prabbles [brabbles, aka petty arguments] and quarrels, and dissensions, and, I warrant you, it is the better for you."

"I want none of your money," John Williams said.

"I give it to you with a good will," Captain Fluellen said. "I can tell you, it will serve you to mend your shoes. Come, take the money. Why should you be so pashful [bashful]? Your shoes is not so good: it is a good silling [shilling], I warrant you, or I will exchange it for one that is good."

John Williams took the money.

An English herald arrived.

Henry V asked him, "Now, herald, have the dead been counted?"

"Here is the number of the slaughtered French," the herald said, handing the King a piece of paper.

Looking at the paper, the King asked Exeter, "What prisoners of noble birth have we taken, uncle?"

Exeter replied, "Charles Duke of Orleans, nephew to the King; John Duke of Bourbon, and Lord Bouciqualt. Of other lords and Barons, Knights and squires, in total fifteen hundred, besides common men."

Henry V said, "This paper tells me that ten thousand French soldiers lie slain in the field. Of this number, Princes and nobles bearing banners with a coat of arms, there lie dead one hundred and twenty-six. In addition, the number of Knights, esquires, and gallant gentlemen who lie dead are eight

housand and four hundred — five hundred of these men were only yesterday
dubbed Knights. In these ten thousand men they have lost, there are only
sixteen hundred paid soldiers; the rest are Princes, Barons, lords, Knights,
squires, and gentlemen of good birth and breeding.

"Here are the names of their nobles who lie dead: Charles Delabreth, High
Constable of France; Jaques of Chatillon, admiral of France; the master of
the cross-bows, Lord Rambures; the Great Master of France, the brave Sir
Guichard Dolphin, John Duke of Alençon; Anthony Duke of Brabant, the
brother of the Duke of Burgundy; and Edward Duke of Bar.

"Here are the names of their powerful Earls who lie dead: Grandpré and
Roussi, Fauconberg and Foix, Beaumont and Marle, Vaudemont and Lestrale.

"Here was a royal fellowship of death!

"Where is the number of our English dead?"

The herald gave him another paper.

Henry V read, "The Duke of York, the Earl of Suffolk, Sir Richard Ketly,
and Davy Gam, esquire — no one else of high rank, and the other casualties
number only twenty-five."

Before the battle, Henry V had sent Davy Gam to scout the number of
enemy soldiers. Davy Gam had reported, "May it please you, my liege, there are
enough to be killed, enough to be taken prisoners, and enough to run away."

Henry V said, "Oh, God, Your arm was here; and not to us, but to Your arm
alone, we owe this victory!

"When, without stratagem, but in straight attack, army against army, and
with fair play in battle, was ever known so great loss on one part and so little
loss on the other? Take all the credit for this victory, God, because it belongs to
You!"

King Henry V was modest here. The English longbows had proved to be
superior weapons in the battle, and the King had devised stratagems to make
very effective use of his archers.

"This victory is wonderful!" Exeter said.

"Come, let's make a procession to the village near the castle of Agincourt.
I now order — on pain of death — all of our soldiers to not boast about this
victory. The credit for this victory belongs to God, and only to God, and I will
not have any soldier take the praise that belongs only to God."

Captain Fluellen asked, "Isn't it lawful and permitted, if it please your majesty, to tell how many soldiers have been killed?"

"Yes, it is, Captain Fluellen," Henry V said, "but only with the acknowledgement: God fought for us."

"Yes, by my conscience, He did us great good," Captain Fluellen said.

Henry V said, "Let us perform all the religious rites. Let the psalms '*Non Nobis*' and '*Te Deum*' be sung. We will enclose the dead in clay — bury them — with Christian charity, and then we will go to Calais and then to England. Never from France have happier men come to England."

CHAPTER 5

Prologue

The Chorus walked on stage and said, "Be kind to those who have not read the biography of King Henry V, and allow me to recap some events of his life. To those of you who have read his biography, I apologize for leaving out of our play events that their length of time, the numbers of people involved, and their magnitude make impossible to cover here on this stage.

"Imagine the King traveling to Calais. Imagine that he has arrived there, and now use your winged thoughts to imagine him traveling across the English Channel. Behold now the English beach fenced in by men, women, and boys — like a wall the throngs of people hold back the sea. The shouts and claps of all these people out-voice the deep-mouthed sea.

"The sea acts like a mighty whiffler — an official who clears a path for the King — and prepares his way to land.

"Having landed, the King journeys on to London.

"So swift a pace has thought that even now you may imagine him at Blackheath, on the road from Dover to London. There his lords try to persuade him to carry his bruised and dented helmet and his bent and hacked sword in a procession in London. Henry V forbids this because he is free from vainness and self-glorious pride; instead, he gives all the tokens and emblems and displays of victory to God, not to himself.

"But now behold in the quick forge and working-house of your thought how London pours out her citizens! The mayor and all his brethren — the aldermen of London — in civil array, similar to the senators of ancient Rome, with the plebeians swarming at their heels, go forth and fetch their conquering Caesar in.

"Imagine a general returning from abroad after putting down a threat to your country. How many citizens would leave the peaceful city so that they could go out and welcome him!

"Many more citizens than that, who had much more cause to rejoice, left London to welcome this Harry.

"Now in London place the King. The French mourn their dead while Henry V stays at home, the Holy Roman Emperor Sigismund visits England to try to arrange peace between England and France, and other events occur that we must omit.

"But now Harry is back in France, so know that he is there.

"I have performed my job of filling in — all too briefly — the gaps. Tolerate my overly brief summary of historical events, and send your thoughts and your eyes to France to see the King."

As the Chorus had said, he had very briefly summarized events. The Battle of Agincourt occurred in 1415, and King Henry V returned to France for the signing of the Treaty of Troyes in 1420.

— 5.1 —

In the English camp, Captain Gower asked Captain Fluellen, "Why are you wearing a leek on your cap today? Saint Davy's day is past."

Captain Fluellen replied, "There is occasions and causes why and wherefore in all things. I will tell you, ass [as] my friend, Captain Gower: The rascally, scald [scurvy], beggarly, lousy, pragging [bragging] knave, Pistol, whom you and yourself and all the world know to be no petter [better] than a fellow, look you now, of no merits, he is come to me and prings [brings] me pread [bread] and salt yesterday, look you, and bid me eat my leek. This happened in a place where I could not fight him, but I will be so bold as to wear a leek in my cap until I see him once again, and then I will tell him a little piece of my desires [mind]."

Pistol walked toward them.

Captain Gower said, "Why, here he comes, swelling like a turkey-cock."

"It is no matter for his swellings nor his turkey-cocks," Captain Fluellen said. "God pless [bless] you, Aunchient [Ancient, aka Ensign] Pistol! You scurvy, bitten-by-louses knave, God pless [bless] you!"

"Ha! Are you bedlam?" Pistol asked. "Are you mad? Do you thirst, base Trojan and hooligan, to have me fold up Parca's fatal web?"

Captain Gower thought, *Pistol is only partially educated, if that. The Parcae — plural — are the Fates, and they cut the thread of life instead of folding up the web of life.*

Pistol blustered, "Hence! Go away! I am qualmish and nauseous at the smell of leek."

Captain Fluellen replied, "I peseech [beseech] you heartily, scurvy, lousy — literally — knave, at my desires, and my requests, and my petitions, to eat, look

102

you, this leek: Because, look you, you do not love it, nor your affections and your appetites and your digestions do not agree with it, and so I would desire you to eat it."

Pistol replied, "Not for Cadwallader and all his goats."

The seventh-century Cadwallader was the last Welsh King to rule Britain. Wales is a mountainous country that is known for its goats, and Pistol was insulting the Welsh by calling them goats.

Captain Fluellen hit Pistol on the head with a cudgel and said, "There is one goat for you."

He then said, "Will you be so good, scauld [scurvy] knave, as to eat this leek?"

"Base Trojan, you shall die," Pistol blustered.

"You say very true, scauld knave. I will die when it is God's will for me to die," Captain Fluellen replied. "I will desire you to live in the meantime, and eat your victuals. Come, here is sauce for it."

Captain Fluellen struck Pistol on the head hard enough with his cudgel for Pistol's blood to flow.

He then said, "You called me yesterday a mountain-squire — a squire of mountainous land of little value — but I will make you today a squire of low degree. I pray you, fall to and eat this meal. If you can mock a leek, you can eat a leek."

"Enough, Captain Fluellen, you have astonished and stunned him," Captain Gower said.

"I say, I will make him eat some part of my leek, or I will peat [beat] his pate [head] four days," Captain Fluellen replied.

He said to Pistol, "Bite, I pray you; it is good for your raw wound and your ploody [bloody] coxcomb, aka foolish head."

Fools, aka jesters, wore a hat resembling a coxcomb.

Pistol asked him, "Must I bite into this leek?"

"Yes, certainly, and out of doubt and out of question, too, and no ambiguities."

Pistol replied, "By this leek, I swear that I will get most horrible revenge —"

Captain Fluellen hit Pistol again with the cudgel and Pistol quickly took a bite of the leek and said, "I'm eating! I'm eating!"

He then muttered, "I swear —"

Captain Fluellen hit him again and said, "Eat, I pray you. Will you have some more sauce for your leek? There is not enough leek to swear by."

"Quiet your cudgel," Pistol said. "You can see that I am eating."

"It will do you much good, scurvy knave — eat heartily. Nay, pray you, throw none away; the skin is good for your broken coxcomb. When you take occasions to see leeks hereafter, I pray you, mock at 'em — I would like to see you do that, really I would."

"You win."

"Ay, leeks is good," Captain Fluellen said. "Wait, here is a groat — fourpence — to heal your pate."

"A whole groat just for me!" Pistol said sarcastically.

"Yes, verily and in truth, you shall take it — or I have another leek in my pocket for you to eat."

"I take your groat as a down payment for my revenge."

"If I owe you anything, I will pay you in cudgels," Captain Fluellen said. "You shall be a seller of wood, and buy nothing from me but wooden cudgels. God be with you, and keep you, and heal your pate."

Captain Fluellen departed.

Pistol said, "All Hell shall stir for this."

Captain Gower said, "No, it won't. You are a false and cowardly knave. Will you mock at an ancient tradition, begun for an honorable reason? The leek is worn on caps as a memorable symbol commemorating long-ago bravery. You have mocked this tradition, but you have not made good with your actions any of your words.

"I have seen you gibing and scoffing at this gentleman, Captain Fluellen, twice or thrice. You thought, because he could not speak English as well as a native Englishman, he could not therefore handle an English cudgel. You have found out otherwise; and henceforth let a Welsh correction teach you good English behavior. Fare you well."

Captain Gower exited.

Alone, Pistol said to himself, "Does Fortune play the hussy with me now and give me only bad luck? I have received news from England that my doll — my wife, Nell — has died in a hospital of the malady of France: venereal disease. No doubt Doll Tearsheet is also dead by now. The inn is lost to me, and therefore I have no refuge. Old do I grow, and from my weary limbs honor is cudgeled. Well, I'll turn pimp, and I will also become a pickpocket with quick hands — I will use a knife to cut the strings of other people's moneybags. I will also get bandages for these cudgeled scars that Fluellen gave to me, and in England I will swear that I got these scars on French battlefields."

— 5.2 —

At the royal palace in France, the English and the French met to establish terms of peace and to sign a peace treaty. In the treaty, Henry V had made many conditions for peace, including his marriage to Katherine, daughter of the French King. He wanted to ensure that his descendants would rule France.

The English people present included King Henry V, Exeter, Bedford, Gloucester, Warwick, Westmoreland, and other Lords. The French people present included the French King, Queen Isabel, the Princess Katherine, Alice (Katherine's attendant, who is older than she), and other ladies. Also present was the mediator, the Duke of Burgundy, and his train. Everyone was very polite and almost everyone was very formal. The highest-ranking royals referred to their counterparts on the other side as close relatives. The Kings also used the royal we.

King Henry V said, "Peace to this meeting — peace is why we have met! To our brother the King of France, and to our sister the Queen of France, I wish health and a good morning. I wish joy and good wishes to our most fair and Princely cousin Katherine. And, as a branch and member of this royalty, by whom this great assembly has been achieved, we do salute you, Duke of Burgundy. Finally, French Princes and peers, health to you all!"

The King of France replied, "Right joyous are we to behold your face, most worthy brother, King of England. You are welcome here, as are all of your English Princes, every one."

"May the outcome of this good day and of this gracious meeting, brother King of England," the Queen of France said, "be happy, as happy as we are now glad to behold your eyes today. Previously, your eyes have opposed the French, who met them in their line of fire. Your eyes were like the fatal eyeballs of murdering basilisks that kill with their looks, and your eyes were like killing cannonballs. Your looks, we sincerely hope, have lost their venomous quality, and we sincerely hope that this day shall change all griefs and quarrels into love."

"I say 'amen' to that," King Henry V said. "That is the reason all of us are here today."

"You English Princes all, I do salute and welcome you," the Queen of France said.

The Duke of Burgundy said, "My duty is to both of you, equally, great Kings of France and England! That I have labored with all my wits, my pains, and my strong endeavors to bring your most imperial majesties to this court of justice and summit conference, your mightiness on both sides best can witness. Since my office has so far prevailed that face to face and royal eye to eye you have greeted each other, let it not disgrace me, if I demand, before this royal view, to know what obstacle or what impediment there is to keep the currently naked, poor, and mangled Peace, that dear nurse of arts and joyful births, from showing her lovely face in this best garden of the world — our fertile France.

"Sadly, Peace has from France too long been chased away. As a result, the crops of France lie in disorder, in heaps, and rotting. France's vines, which produce wine, the merry cheerer of the heart, die from lack of pruning and lack of care. France's formerly trimmed hedges are like prisoners with wildly overgrown hair; they put forth disordered twigs. France's arable land now lies unplowed, and on it grows only weeds such as the darnel, hemlock, and rank fumitory. The plows that should uproot such wild and savage weeds rust. The level meadows that formerly brought sweetly forth desirable plants such as the freckled cowslip, burnet, and green clover now lack the farmers who wield the scythe. Because the meadows lack horticultural care, they are all uncultivated and rank; in them wild weeds grow, and nothing breeds except hateful dock-leaves, rough thistles, dry hollow stalks, and burs, none of which have beauty or utility.

"And just as our vineyards, arable land now lying fallow, meadows, and hedges, defective in their natures, grow wild, our families and ourselves and our children have forgotten, or do not learn because of lack of time, the sciences that should civilize our country; instead, they become like savages — as soldiers will who do nothing except think about bloodshed. They swear and give stern looks, wear ragged clothing, and are accustomed to everything that seems unnatural.

"Therefore, you are here today so that we can bring Peace and the blessings of Peace back and we can return to the good things that we once had. I ask you to let me know why gentle Peace should not expel these evils that I have mentioned and bless us again."

King Henry V said, "If, Duke of Burgundy, you would have the Peace you want, whose lack gives growth to the imperfections that you have cited, you must buy that Peace by getting full agreement to all our just demands, whose general aims and specific details are briefly summarized in the document you are holding in your hands."

The Duke of Burgundy replied, "The King of France has heard your demands, but he has not yet replied to them."

King Henry V said, "Well, then, whether there shall be Peace, which you have been advocating, lies in his answer to our demands."

The King of France said, "I have only cursorily glanced over your demands. If it pleases your grace to appoint some of your council immediately to sit and meet with us once more, so that we can with better heed consider your demands, we will quickly let you know to which Articles of Peace we agree."

"Brother, we shall do that," Henry V said. "Go, uncle Exeter, and brother Clarence, and you, too, brother Gloucester, Warwick and Huntingdon, go with the King of France. And take with you complete power to ratify, augment, or alter our demands, as your wisdoms best shall see advantageous for our dignity. We will sign what you agree to."

He then said to the Queen of France, "Will you, fair sister, go with the Princes, or stay here with us?"

"Our gracious brother, I will go with them. Perhaps a woman's voice may do some good, when arguments over the Articles of Peace are unnecessarily made."

Henry V requested, "Allow our cousin Katherine to stay here with us. My marriage to her is our capital demand; it is among the first things listed in the treaty."

"She has permission to stay," the Queen of France replied.

Everyone except King Henry V and Katherine — and Alice, her attendant and chaperone — exited.

Henry V and Katherine were going to be married; Henry V knew it, and Katherine knew it. That is why Katherine had been learning to speak English. But simply telling a woman that you are going to marry her so that your heirs can become King of France is no way to treat a lady, and so Henry V wooed Katherine, although she spoke little English and he spoke little French.

Henry V said, "Lovely and most beautiful Katherine, will you be so kind as to teach a soldier terms such as will enter a lady's ear and plead his love to her gentle heart?"

"Your majesty shall mock at me," Katherine said. "I cannot speak your England."

"Oh, lovely Katherine, if you will love me soundly with your French heart, I will be glad to hear you confess it brokenly with your English tongue. Do you like me, Kate?"

"*Pardonnez-moi* [Pardon me], I cannot tell vat is 'like me.'"

"An angel is like you, Kate, and you are like an angel."

Katherine asked Alice, her attendant and chaperone, "*Que dit-il? Que je suis semblable a les anges*? [What did he say? That I am like the angels?]"

Alice replied, "*Oui, vraiment, sauf votre grace, ainsi dit-il.* [Yes, really, begging your grace's pardon, that is what he said.]"

"I said so, lovely Katherine," Henry V said, "and I must not blush to affirm it."

Katherine said, "*Oh, bon Dieu! Les langues des hommes sont pleines de trumperies*! [Oh, good God! The tongues of men are full of deceits!]"

Henry V asked Alice, "What says she, fair one? That the tongues of men are full of deceits?"

Alice replied, "*Oui* [Yes], dat de tongues of de mans is be full of deceits: dat is say de Princess."

"The Princess is the better Englishwoman because she prefers plain speaking," Henry V said. "Truly, Kate, my wooing is fit for your understanding: I am glad you can speak no better English; for, if you could, you would find me such a plain King that you would think I had been a farmer and had sold my farm to buy my crown. I know no ways to mince it in love — to speak like a courtier — so instead I will directly and openly say, 'I love you.' If you press me any farther than to reply, 'Do you truly love me?' then I have no fancy words to say and so my courtship is over. Give me your answer. Please, do. Say you will marry me and we will shake hands and so make a bargain. What have you to say, lady?"

Katherine replied, "*Sauf votre honneur* [Saving your grace], me understand vell."

Henry V said, "By the Virgin Mary, if you want me to write love verses or to dance to court you, Kate, why, then you undo me. As far as writing poetry is concerned, I have neither words nor meter, and as far as dancing is concerned, I have no strength in measuring dance steps, yet I have a reasonable measure of strength. If I could win a lady by playing leapfrog, or by vaulting into my saddle with my armor on my back, I can say without bragging that I should quickly leap into a wife."

He thought, *And leap onto a wife in bed.*

He continued, "Or if I could fist-fight for my love, or if I could make my horse leap for her favors, I would hit like a butcher felling a beast before butchering it and I would sit on a horse like a specially trained ape and never fall off. But, before God, Kate, I cannot look like a love-sick youth or gasp out eloquent love-talk — I have no skill in professing my love for you. I have only downright oaths, which I never make until urged to, and which I never break even when urged to.

"If you can love a fellow of this temper, Kate, whose face is not worth being sunburned because it is already brown and cannot become uglier, who never looks in his mirror because of love of anything he sees there, let your eye be your cook — let it make me appear to be the way that you want me to be. Garnish me to make me more attractive than I am.

"I speak to you like a plain soldier. If you can love me for this — what I am — take me. If you will not marry me, to say to you that I shall die is true, but I will not die because I lack your love, by God. Yet it is true that I love you.

"While you live, dear Kate, take a fellow of plain and natural constancy because he must do you right, because he has not the gift to woo in other places: These fellows of infinite tongue, who can talk well and make rhymes and win the love of many women, end up talking themselves out of love again.

"Listen! A speaker is only a prattler; a rhyme is only a song that will not be long remembered. A good leg will waste away; a straight back will stoop; a black beard will turn white; a pate with curled hair will grow bald; a fair face will wither; a full eye will grow hollow. But a good heart, Kate, is the Sun and the Moon; or, rather, it is the Sun and not the Moon because it shines brightly and never changes, but keeps its course truly. If you would have such a one, then take me. If you take me, you will take a soldier, and if you take a soldier, then you take a King. And what do you say now to my love? Speak, my lovely lady, and give me the answer I want to hear, please."

Katherine replied, "Is it possible dat I sould [should] love de enemy of France?"

"No, it is not possible that you should love the enemy of France, Kate," Henry V said, "but, in loving me, you would love the friend of France because I love France so well that I will not part with even one village of it. I will have all of France, and, Kate, when France is mine and I am yours, then France is yours and you are mine."

"I cannot tell vat is dat," Katherine replied.

"No, Kate?" Henry V said. "I will tell you in French, which I am sure will hang upon my tongue like a new-married wife about her husband's neck, hardly to be shook off.

"*Je quand sur le possession de France, et quand vous avez le possession de moi* [I still on the possession of France, and when you have possession of me] — let me see, what then? Saint Denis, patron saint of France, help me! — *donc votre est France et vous etes mienne* [so yours is France and you are mine].

"It is as easy for me, Kate, to conquer the Kingdom of France as it would be to speak so much more French. I shall never move you in French, unless it be to move you to laugh at me."

Katherine replied, "*Sauf votre honneur, le Francois que vous parlez, il est meilleur que l'Anglois lequel je parle.* [With respect, the French you speak is better than the English I speak.]"

"No, truly, it is not, Kate," Henry V said, "but your speaking in my tongue, and I in yours, most truly-falsely — true in meaning but incorrect in grammar — must be granted to be very much at the same skill level. But, Kate, do you understand as much English as will allow you to understand and answer this question — can you love me?"

"I cannot tell."

"Can any of your neighbors tell, Kate? I'll ask them. Come, I know you love me. At night, when you go into your bedroom, you'll question this gentlewoman — Alice — about me, and I know, Kate, to her you will criticize those parts in me that you love with your heart. But, good Kate, mock me mercifully; do this, gentle Princess, because I love you terribly.

"If ever you are mine, Kate, as I have faith that you will be, I will get you with struggling as if I were in a battle, and you will therefore prove to be the mother of good soldiers. Shall not you and I, with the help of Saint Denis and Saint George, create a boy, half French and half English, who shall go to Constantinople and take the Turk by the beard in a Crusade? Shall we not? What have you to say about that, my fair flower-*de-luce* [he meant *fleur-de-lis*, aka the French heraldic lily]?"

"I do not know dat," Katherine said.

"No," Henry V said, "you do not know that now. Hereafter you shall know, but now is the time to promise."

Henry V thought, *The Biblical "knowing" will occur after we are married. We will have a son. We need to produce an heir.*

He added, "Promise me now, Kate, that you will endeavor to do your part in producing the French part of such a boy; as for my English moiety, aka half, take the word of a King and a bachelor. What is your answer, *la plus belle Catherine du monde, mon tres cher et devin deesse* [the most beautiful Katherine in the world and my very dear and divine goddess]?"

"Your majestee 'ave *fausse* [false, inaccurate, deceiving] French enough to deceive de most *sage demoiselle* [wise lady] dat is en France," Katherine replied.

"A plague upon my false French!" Henry V said. "By my honor, in true English, I love you, Kate. By my honor, I dare not swear you love me, yet my passion begins to flatter me that you do, notwithstanding the poor and discouraging effect of my looks.

"Curse my father's ambition! He was thinking of civil wars when he got my mother pregnant with me. My father's thoughts when I was conceived had an effect on me. Because of my father's thoughts, I was created with a stubborn outside, with an aspect or appearance of iron, with the result that, when I attempt to woo ladies, I frighten them.

"But, truly, Kate, the older I grow, the better I shall appear. My comfort is that old age, which badly treats beauty, can do nothing more to spoil my face — I am already ugly.

"You will have me, if you will have me, at the worst, and you will see that I will grow better and better the longer you have and enjoy me.

"Therefore, tell me, most lovely Katherine, will you have me? Will you marry me? Put away your maiden blushes; instead, give expression to the thoughts of your heart with the looks of an Empress. Take me by the hand, and say to me, 'Harry of England, I am yours.'

"As soon as you say those blessed words to me, I will tell you out loud, 'England is yours, Ireland is yours, France is yours, and Harry Plantagenet — me — is yours.'

"Harry Plantagenet is a person who, though I speak it to his face, if he not fellow with — that is, equal to — the best King, you shall find that he is the best King of good fellows.

"Come, tell me your answer in broken music; for your voice is music and your English is broken; therefore, Queen of all, Katherine, tell your mind to me in broken English; will you have me and marry me?"

"Dat is as it sall [shall] please de *roi mon pere* [the King my father]."

"It will please him well, Kate," Henry V said. "It shall please him, Kate."

Henry V knew that the King of France would sign the peace treaty.

"Den it sall also please me."

"Hearing that, I now kiss your hand, and I call you my Queen."

Henry V took her hand so that he could kiss it.

Katherine replied, "*Laissez, mon seigneur, laissez, laissez! Ma foi, je ne veux point que vous abaissiez votre grandeur en baisant la main d'une de votre seigeurie indigne serviteur! Excusez-moi, je vous supplie, mon tres-puissant seigneur.*"

[Katherine replied, "Let go, my lord, let go, let go! On my word, I would never wish you to lower your dignity by kissing the hand of an unworthy servant of your majesty! Pardon me, I beg you, my most mighty lord."]

"Then I will kiss your lips, Kate."

Katherine replied, "*Les dames et demoiselles pour etre baisees devant leur noces, il n'est pas la coutume de France.*"

[Katherine replied, "It is not the custom for women and maidens to be kissed before they are married."]

Those of you who understand that *baisees* means both "kissed" and, colloquially, "f**ked" may laugh now.

Henry V asked Alice, "Madam my interpreter, what is she saying?"

"Dat it is not be de fashion pour les ladies of France — I cannot tell vat is *baiser* en Anglish."

"To kiss," Henry V said.

Alice replied, "Your majesty *entendre bettre que moi* [understands better than me]."

You may now laugh at the word "*entendre.*"

"Does she say that it is not a fashion for the maidens in France to kiss before they are married?" Henry V asked.

Alice replied, "*Oui, vraiment.* [Yes, really.]"

Henry V said, "Overly strict customs bow before great Kings. Dear Kate, you and I cannot be confined within the weak rules of a country's fashion. We are the makers of manners, Kate, and the liberty that comes with high positions stops the mouth of all find-faults. You have upheld the overly strict fashion of your country by denying me a kiss, and therefore I will stop your mouth with a kiss. Therefore, be patient and yielding."

He kissed her and said, "You have witchcraft in your lips, Kate. There is more eloquence in a sugar-sweet touch of your lips than in the tongues of the French council; and your lips should sooner persuade Harry of England than a petition of all the Kings in the world."

He heard a noise and said, "Here comes your father."

The King and Queen of France, Burgundy, and other lords entered the room.

"God save your majesty!" Burgundy said, "My royal cousin, are you teaching our French Princess English?"

"I would have her learn, my fair kinsman, how perfectly I love her," Henry V said, "and that is good English."

"Is she not eager and willing to learn?" Burgundy asked.

"Our English tongue, aka language, is rough, kinsman, and my behavior is not smooth," Henry V said, "so that, having neither the voice nor the heart of flattery about me, I cannot conjure up the spirit of love in her so that the spirit of love will appear in his true likeness."

Burgundy, who enjoyed bawdy puns and humor, said, "Pardon the frankness of my jokes as I give you advice for your problem. If you would conjure in her, you must make a circle."

Henry V thought, *To conjure is to raise, and in the act of sex the part of a man that is raised must make a circle as it penetrates a vagina.*

Burgundy continued, "If you conjure up Love, aka Cupid, in her in his true likeness, he must appear naked and blind because in art Cupid usually appears blindfolded and naked."

Henry V thought, *A penis is naked and blind when it penetrates a vagina, whose inside is dark.*

Burgundy continued, "Can you blame her then, being a maid yet rosed over with the virgin crimson of modesty — a blush — if she deny the appearance of a naked blind boy in her naked seeing self?"

Henry V thought, *Many virgins blush when a naked penis approaches a naked and exposed-to-light c*nt.*

Burgundy continued, "It were, my lord, a hard condition for a maiden to yield to."

Henry V thought, *Yes, the penis must be in a hard condition in such a situation.*

He said to Burgundy, "Yet maidens do close their eyes and yield, as love is blind and enforces."

Burgundy thought, *"Enforces" is a good word here because the penis forces, aka pushes, its way into a vagina, where the penis is blind in the dark.*

Burgundy said, "They are then excused, my lord, when they see not what they do."

Henry V thought, *They — maidens and vaginas — are excused because they see not what they do.*

He said to Burgundy, "Then, my good lord, teach your cousin Katherine to consent and wink."

Burgundy thought, *"Consent" means to consent to love and marry him, and it means to consent to have sex with him. The word "wink" can mean to close one's eyes.*

Burgundy said, "I will wink at Katherine to let her know that she should consent, my lord, if you will teach her to know my meaning."

Henry V thought, *"Teach her to know my meaning" means to teach her about sex.*

Burgundy continued, "Virgins, well summered, aka well taken care of, and with warm blood, are like flies on Saint Bartholomew's Day — August 24. They are blind, though they have their eyes; and then they will endure handling, which before would not abide looking on."

Henry V thought, *Flies are supposed to be so sluggish on Saint Bartholomew's Day that it is as if they were blind and so they can be easily caught. In late summer, virgins who have warm blood — are in heat — close their eyes and allow themselves to be caught and handled.*

Henry V said, "This moral ties me over to time and a hot summer; and so I shall catch the fly, your cousin, in the latter end and she must be blind, too."

Burgundy thought, *The marriage of Henry V and Katherine will take place in summer. She will close her eyes, and he will "catch" her end.*

Burgundy said, "Blind — as love is, my lord, before it loves. Love is blind, my lord, before it begins truly to love."

Henry V said, "That is true, and you may, some of you, thank love for my blindness. I cannot see many a fair French city because of one beautiful French maiden — Katherine — who stands in my way."

The King of France said, "My lord, you see the fair French cities, but you see them from a different perspective than is usual. For you, the cities are turned into a maiden because they are all girdled with maiden walls that war has never entered."

Henry V thought, *Enough sex puns and metaphors.*

He asked the King of France, "Shall Kate be my wife?"

"Yes, if you want to marry her."

"I do," Henry V said, "as long as the maiden cities you talk about will serve as her dowry. That way, the maiden who stood in the way of what I wish shall be the way for me to get what I wish."

The King of France said, "We have consented to all reasonable terms."

Henry V asked, "Is that true, my lords of England?"

Westmoreland replied, "The King has granted every Article of Peace. He has granted his daughter first, and then following that he has granted all the rest of the things that you definitely wanted."

Exeter said, "There is one thing that he has not agreed to.

"Your majesty demanded that the King of France, when he has any occasion to write to you about grants of land and titles, shall refer to your highness in this way and with this title in French: *Notre trescher fils Henri, Roi d'Angleterre, Heritier de France* [Our very dear son Henry, King of England and Heir to France].

"You also wanted him when writing you to refer to your highness in this way and with this title in Latin: *Praecarissimus filius noster Henricus, Rex Angliae, et Haeres Franciae* [Our very dear son Henry, King of England and Heir to France]."

The King of France said, "I am also willing to agree to this, brother, if you request me to do so."

Henry V said, "I request you then, in love and dear alliance, to agree to that article along with the rest, and thereupon give me your daughter."

"Take her, fair son," the King of France said, "and have children with her so that the contending Kingdoms of France and England, whose very shores — and white cliffs — look pale with envy of each other's happiness, may cease their hatred, and this dear conjunction of English King and French Princess may plant neighborliness and Christian-like accord in the sweet bosoms of the English citizens and the French citizens, so that never again will war advance its blood-dripping sword between England and fair France."

Everyone present said, "Amen!"

Henry V said, "Now, welcome, Kate: and all of you bear witness that here and now I kiss her as my sovereign Queen."

The Queen of France said, "May God, Who is the best maker of all marriages, combine your hearts in one, and your realms in one! As man and wife, being two, are one in love, so let there be between your Kingdoms such a marriage that never may wrongdoing, or cruel jealousy, which trouble often the bed of blessed marriage, thrust in between the compact of these Kingdoms, to separate their union in one body. May the Englishmen be Frenchmen, and may the Frenchmen be Englishmen, and may they so treat each other. May God say 'Amen!' — 'So be it!' — to this."

Everyone present said, "Amen!"

King Henry V said, "Now we will prepare for our marriage — on which day, my Lord of Burgundy, we'll take your oath, and all the peers' oaths, for security of our alliance. Then I shall swear to Kate —" he looked at her "— and Kate to me; and may our oaths well kept and prosperous be!"

EPILOGUE

The Chorus appeared and said, "Thus far in history, with rough and all-unable and all-unskilled pen, our author, bending over his writing desk, has pursued his story, confining important people such as the King of England and the King of France in a little book and on a little stage, mangling in fits and starts the full course of their glory.

"This star of England — King Henry V — lived only a short time, but in that short time he most greatly lived and accomplished much. Good fortune followed him in war, by which he conquered France, the world's best garden, and he left France to his imperial son.

"His infant son, Henry VI, was crowned King of England and King of France. But so many people were involved in managing the young King's affairs that they lost France and made his England bleed with civil war. Our stage has often told this tale in productions of the three plays of *Henry VI*.

"For the sake of those three plays, we hope that you will kindly receive — and applaud — this play."

APPENDIX A: BRIEF HISTORICAL BACKGROUND

KING EDWARD I: 1272-1307

Edward Longshanks fought and defeated the Welsh chieftains, and he made his eldest son the Prince of Wales. He won victories against the Scots, and he brought the coronation stone from Scone to Westminster.

KING EDWARD II: 1307-deposed 1327

At the Battle of Bannockburn in 1314, the Scots defeated his army. His wife and her lover, Mortimer, deposed him. According to legend, he was murdered in Berkeley Castle by means of a red-hot poker thrust up his anus.

KING EDWARD III: 1327-1377

Son of King Edward II, he reigned for a long time — 50 years. Because he wanted to conquer Scotland and France, he started the Hundred Years War in 1338. King Edward III and his eldest son, Edward the Black Prince, won important victories against the French in the Battle of Crécy (1346) and the Battle of Poitiers (1356).

One of King Edward III's sons was John of Gaunt, first Duke of Lancaster.

Another of King Edward III's sons was Edmund of Langley, first Duke of York.

During his reign, the Black Death — the bubonic plague — struck in 1348-1350 and killed half of England's population.

KING RICHARD II: 1377-deposed 1399

King Richard II was the son of Edward the Black Prince. In 1381, Wat Tyler led the Peasants Revolt, which was suppressed. King Richard II sent Henry, Duke of Lancaster, into exile and seized Henry's estates, but in 1399 Henry, Duke of Lancaster, returned from exile and deposed King Richard II, thereby becoming King Henry IV. In 1400, King Richard II was murdered in Pontefract Castle, which is also known as Pomfret Castle.

HOUSE OF LANCASTER

KING HENRY IV: 1399-1413

Henry, Duke of Lancaster, was the son of John of Gaunt, who was the third son of King Edward III. He was born at Bolingbroke Castle and so was also known as Henry of Bolingbroke. Returning from exile in France to reclaim his estates, he deposed King Richard II. He spent the 13 years of his reign putting down rebellions and defending himself against those who would assassinate or depose him. The Welshman Owen Glendower and the English Percy family were among those who fought against him. King Henry IV died at the age of 45.

KING HENRY V: 1413-1422

The son of King Henry IV, King Henry V renewed the war with France. He and his army defeated the French at the Battle of Agincourt (1415) despite being heavily outnumbered. He married Catherine of Valoise, the daughter of the French King, but he died before becoming King of France. He left behind a 10-month-old son, who became King Henry VI.

KING HENRY VI: 1422-deposed 1461; briefly returned to the throne in 1470-1471

The Hundred Years War ended in 1453; the English lost all land in France except for Calais, a port city. After King Henry VI suffered an attack of mental illness in 1454, Richard, third Duke of York and the father of King Henry IV and King Richard III, was made Protector of the Realm. England suffered civil war after the House of York challenged King Henry VI's right to be King of England. In 1470, King Henry VI was briefly restored to the English throne. In 1471, he was murdered in the Tower of London. A short time previously, his son, Edward, Prince of Wales, had been killed at the Battle of Tewkesbury in 1471; this was the final battle in the War of the Roses. The Yorkists decisively defeated the Lancastrians.

King Henry VI founded both Eton College and King's College, Cambridge.

WAR OF THE ROSES

From 1455-1487, the Yorkists and the Lancastrians fought for power in England in the famous War of the Roses. The emblem of the York family was a white rose, and the emblem of the Lancaster family was a red rose. The Yorkists and the Lancastrians were descended from King Edward III.

HOUSE OF YORK

KING EDWARD IV: 1461-1483 (King Henry VI briefly returned to the throne in 1470-1471)

Son of Richard, third Duke of York, he charged his brother George, Duke of Clarence, with treason and had him murdered in 1478. After dying suddenly, he left behind two sons aged 12 and 9, and five daughters.

His surviving two brothers in Shakespeare's play *Richard III* are these: 1) George, Duke of Clarence. Clarence is the second-oldest brother; and 2) Richard, Duke of Gloucester, and afterwards King Richard III. Gloucester is the youngest surviving brother.

William Caxton established the first printing press in Westminster during King Edward IV's reign.

KING EDWARD V: 1483-1483

The eldest son of King Edward IV, he reigned for only two months, the shortest-lived monarch in English history. He was 13 years old. He and his younger brother, Richard, were murdered in the Tower of London. According to Shakespeare's play, their uncle, Richard, Duke of Gloucester, who became King Richard III, was responsible for their murders.

KING RICHARD III: 1483-1485

Brother of King Edward IV, Richard, the Duke of Gloucester, declared the two Princes in the Tower of London — King Edward V and Richard, Duke of York — illegitimate and made himself King Richard III. In 1485, Henry Tudor, Earl of Richmond, a descendant of John of Gaunt, who was the father of King Henry IV, defeated King Richard III at the Battle of Bosworth Field in Leicestershire. King Richard III died in that battle.

King Richard III's father was Richard Plantagenet, Duke of York. His mother was Cecily Neville, Duchess of York.

King Richard III's death in the Battle of Bosworth Field is regarded as marking the end of the Middle Ages in England.

A NOTE ON THE PLANTAGENETS

The first Plantagenet King was King Henry II (1154-1189). From 1154 until 1485, when King Richard III died, all English kings were Plantagenets. Both the Lancaster family and the York family were Plantagenets.

Geoffrey Plantagenet, Count of Anjou, was the founder of the House of Plantagenet. Geoffrey's son, Henry Curtmantle, became King Henry II of England, thereby founding the Plantagenet dynasty. Geoffrey wore a sprig of broom, a flowering shrub, as a badge; the Latin name for broom is *planta genista,* and from it the name "Plantagenet" arose.

The Plantagenet dynasty can be divided into three parts:

1154-1216: The Angevins. The Angevin Kings were Henry II, Richard I (Richard the Lionheart), and John 1.

1216-1399: The Plantagenets. These Kings ranged from King Henry III to King Richard II.

1399-1485: The Houses of Lancaster and of York. These Kings ranged from King Henry IV to King Richard III.

BEGINNING OF THE TUDOR DYNASTY

KING HENRY VII: 1485-1509

When King Richard III fell at the Battle of Bosworth, Henry Tudor, Earl of Richmond, became King Henry VII. A Lancastrian, he married Elizabeth of York — young Elizabeth of York in *Richard III* — and united the two warring houses, York and Lancaster, thus ending the War of the Roses. One of his grandfathers was Sir Owen Tudor, who married Catherine of Valoise, widow of King Henry V.

KING HENRY VIII: 1509-1547

King Henry VIII had six wives. These are their fates: "Divorced, Beheaded, Died, Divorced, Beheaded, Survived." He divorced his first wife, Catherine of Aragon, so that he could marry Anne Boleyn. Because of this, England divorced itself from the Catholic Church, and King Henry VIII became the head of the Church of England. King Henry VIII had one son and two daughters, all of whom became rulers of England: Edward, daughter of Jane Seymour; Mary, daughter of Catherine of Aragon; and Elizabeth, daughter of Anne Boleyn.

KING EDWARD VI: 1547-1553

The son of Henry VIII and Jane Seymour, King Edward VI succeeded his father at the age of nine; a Council of Regency with his uncle, Duke of Somerset, styled Protector, ruled the government.

During King Edward VI's reign, Archbishop Thomas Cranmer wrote the 1549 Book of Common Prayer.

When King Edward VI died, Lady Jane Grey was proclaimed Queen, but she ruled for only nine days before being executed in 1554, aged 17. Mary, daughter of Catherine of Aragon, became Queen. She was Catholic, thus the attempt to make Lady Jane Grey, a Protestant, Queen.

QUEEN MARY I (BLOODY MARY) 1553-1558

Queen Mary I attempted to make England a Catholic nation again. Some Protestant bishops, including Archbishop Thomas Cranmer, were burnt at the stake, and other violence broke out, resulting in her being known as Bloody Mary.

QUEEN ELIZABETH I: 1558-1603

The daughter of King Henry VIII and Anne Boleyn, Queen Elizabeth I was a popular Queen. In 1588, the English navy decisively defeated the Spanish Armada. England had many notable playwrights and poets, including William Shakespeare and Ben Jonson, during her reign. She never married and had no children.

KING JAMES I OF ENGLAND: A MEMBER OF THE HOUSE OF STUART

KING JAMES I OF ENGLAND AND VI OF SCOTLAND: 1603-1625

King James I of England was the son of Mary, Queen of Scots, and Lord Darnley. In 1605 Guy Fawkes and his Catholic co-conspirators were captured before they could blow up the Houses of Parliament; this was known as the Gunpowder Plot.

In 1611, during King James I's reign, the Authorized Version of the Bible (the King James Version) was completed.

Also during King James I's reign, in 1620 the Pilgrims sailed for America in their ship *The Mayflower*.

A NOTE ON SHAKESPEARE

William Shakespeare lived under two monarchs: Queen Elizabeth I and King James I.

APPENDIX B: ABOUT THE AUTHOR

was a dark and stormy night. Suddenly a cry rang out, and on a hot summer night in 1954, Josephine, wife of Carl Bruce, gave birth to a boy — me. Unfortunately, this young married couple allowed Reuben Saturday, Josephine's brother, to name their first-born. Reuben, aka "The Joker," decided that Bruce was a nice name, so he decided to name me Bruce Bruce. I have gone by my middle name — David — ever since.

Being named Bruce David Bruce hasn't been all bad. Bank tellers remember me very quickly, so I don't often have to show an ID. It can be fun in charades, also. When I was a counselor as a teenager at Camp Echoing Hills in Warsaw, Ohio, a fellow counselor gave the signs for "sounds like" and "two words," then she pointed to a bruise on her leg twice. Bruise bruise? Oh yeah, Bruce Bruce is the answer!

Uncle Reuben, by the way, gave me a haircut when I was in kindergarten. He cut my hair short and shaved a small bald spot on the back of my head. My mother wouldn't let me go to school until the bald spot grew out again.

Of all my brothers and sisters (six in all), I am the only transplant to Athens, Ohio. I was born in Newark, Ohio, and have lived all around Southeastern Ohio. However, I moved to Athens to go to Ohio University and have never left.

At Ohio U, I never could make up my mind whether to major in English or Philosophy, so I got a bachelor's degree with a double major in both areas, then I added a master's degree in English and a master's degree in Philosophy.

Currently, and for a long time to come (I eat fruits and vegetables), I am spending my retirement writing books such as *Nadia Comaneci: Perfect 10*, *The Funniest People in Dance*, *Homer's* Iliad: *A Retelling in Prose*, and *William Shakespeare's* Othello: *A Retelling in Prose*.

By the way, my sister Brenda Kennedy writes romances such as *A New Beginning* and *Shattered Dreams*.

APPENDIX C: SOME BOOKS BY DAVID BRUCE

Retellings of a Classic Work of Literature

Arden of Faversham: A Retelling

Ben Jonson's The Alchemist: *A Retelling*

Ben Jonson's The Arraignment, or Poetaster: *A Retelling*

Ben Jonson's Bartholomew Fair: *A Retelling*

Ben Jonson's The Case is Altered: *A Retelling*

Ben Jonson's Catiline's Conspiracy: *A Retelling*

Ben Jonson's The Devil is an Ass: *A Retelling*

Ben Jonson's Epicene: *A Retelling*

Ben Jonson's Every Man in His Humor: *A Retelling*

Ben Jonson's Every Man Out of His Humor: *A Retelling*

Ben Jonson's The Fountain of Self-Love, or Cynthia's Revels: *A Retelling*

Ben Jonson's The Magnetic Lady, or Humors Reconciled: *A Retelling*

Ben Jonson's The New Inn, or The Light Heart: *A Retelling*

Ben Jonson's Sejanus' Fall: *A Retelling*

Ben Jonson's The Staple of News: *A Retelling*

Ben Jonson's A Tale of a Tub: *A Retelling*

Ben Jonson's Volpone, or the Fox: *A Retelling*

Christopher Marlowe's Complete Plays: Retellings

Christopher Marlowe's Dido, Queen of Carthage: *A Retelling*

Christopher Marlowe's Doctor Faustus: *Retellings of the 1604 A-Text and of the 1616 B-Text*

Christopher Marlowe's Edward II: *A Retelling*

Christopher Marlowe's The Massacre at Paris: *A Retelling*

Christopher Marlowe's The Rich Jew of Malta: *A Retelling*

Christopher Marlowe's Tamburlaine, Parts 1 and 2: *Retellings*

Dante's Divine Comedy: *A Retelling in Prose*

Dante's Inferno: *A Retelling in Prose*

Dante's Purgatory: *A Retelling in Prose*

Dante's Paradise: *A Retelling in Prose*

The Famous Victories of Henry V: A Retelling

From the Iliad *to the* Odyssey: *A Retelling in Prose of Quintus of Smyrna's* Posthomerica

George Chapman, Ben Jonson, and John Marston's Eastward Ho! *A Retelling*

George Peele's The Arraignment of Paris: *A Retelling*

George Peele's The Battle of Alcazar: *A Retelling*

George Peele's David and Bathsheba, and the Tragedy of Absalom: *A Retelling*

George Peele's Edward I: *A Retelling*

George Peele's The Old Wives' Tale: *A Retelling*

George-a-Greene: *A Retelling*

The History of King Leir: *A Retelling*

Homer's Iliad: *A Retelling in Prose*

Homer's Odyssey: *A Retelling in Prose*

J.W. Gent.'s The Valiant Scot: *A Retelling*

Jason and the Argonauts: A Retelling in Prose of Apollonius of Rhodes' Argonautica

John Ford: Eight Plays Translated into Modern English

John Ford's The Broken Heart: *A Retelling*

John Ford's The Fancies, Chaste and Noble: *A Retelling*

John Ford's The Lady's Trial: *A Retelling*

John Ford's The Lover's Melancholy: *A Retelling*

John Ford's Love's Sacrifice: *A Retelling*

John Ford's Perkin Warbeck: *A Retelling*

John Ford's The Queen: *A Retelling*

John Ford's 'Tis Pity She's a Whore: *A Retelling*

John Lyly's Campaspe: *A Retelling*

John Lyly's Endymion, The Man in the Moon: *A Retelling*

John Lyly's Galatea: *A Retelling*

John Lyly's Love's Metamorphosis: *A Retelling*

John Lyly's Midas: *A Retelling*

John Lyly's Mother Bombie: *A Retelling*

John Lyly's Sappho and Phao: *A Retelling*

John Lyly's The Woman in the Moon: *A Retelling*

John Webster's The White Devil: *A Retelling*

King Edward III: *A Retelling*

Mankind: *A Medieval Morality Play* (A Retelling)

Margaret Cavendish's The Unnatural Tragedy: *A Retelling*

The Merry Devil of Edmonton: *A Retelling*

The Summoning of Everyman: *A Medieval Morality Play* (A Retelling)

Robert Greene's Friar Bacon and Friar Bungay: *A Retelling*

The Taming of a Shrew: *A Retelling*

Tarlton's Jests: A Retelling

Thomas Middleton's A Chaste Maid in Cheapside: *A Retelling*

Thomas Middleton's Women Beware Women: *A Retelling*

Thomas Middleton and Thomas Dekker's The Roaring Girl: *A Retelling*

Thomas Middleton and William Rowley's The Changeling: *A Retelling*

The Trojan War and Its Aftermath: Four Ancient Epic Poems

Virgil's Aeneid: *A Retelling in Prose*

William Shakespeare's 5 Late Romances: Retellings in Prose

William Shakespeare's 10 Histories: Retellings in Prose

William Shakespeare's 11 Tragedies: Retellings in Prose

William Shakespeare's 12 Comedies: Retellings in Prose

William Shakespeare's 38 Plays: Retellings in Prose
William Shakespeare's 1 Henry IV, aka Henry IV, Part 1: *A Retelling in Prose*
William Shakespeare's 2 Henry IV, aka Henry IV, Part 2: *A Retelling in Prose*
William Shakespeare's 1 Henry VI, aka Henry VI, Part 1: *A Retelling in Prose*
William Shakespeare's 2 Henry VI, aka Henry VI, Part 2: *A Retelling in Prose*
William Shakespeare's 3 Henry VI, aka Henry VI, Part 3: *A Retelling in Prose*
William Shakespeare's All's Well that Ends Well: *A Retelling in Prose*
William Shakespeare's Antony and Cleopatra: *A Retelling in Prose*
William Shakespeare's As You Like It: *A Retelling in Prose*
William Shakespeare's The Comedy of Errors: *A Retelling in Prose*
William Shakespeare's Coriolanus: *A Retelling in Prose*
William Shakespeare's Cymbeline: *A Retelling in Prose*
William Shakespeare's Hamlet: *A Retelling in Prose*
William Shakespeare's Henry V: *A Retelling in Prose*
William Shakespeare's Henry VIII: *A Retelling in Prose*
William Shakespeare's Julius Caesar: *A Retelling in Prose*
William Shakespeare's King John: *A Retelling in Prose*
William Shakespeare's King Lear: *A Retelling in Prose*
William Shakespeare's Love's Labor's Lost: *A Retelling in Prose*
William Shakespeare's Macbeth: *A Retelling in Prose*
William Shakespeare's Measure for Measure: *A Retelling in Prose*
William Shakespeare's The Merchant of Venice: *A Retelling in Prose*
William Shakespeare's The Merry Wives of Windsor: *A Retelling in Prose*
William Shakespeare's A Midsummer Night's Dream: *A Retelling in Prose*
William Shakespeare's Much Ado About Nothing: *A Retelling in Prose*
William Shakespeare's Othello: *A Retelling in Prose*
William Shakespeare's Pericles, Prince of Tyre: *A Retelling in Prose*
William Shakespeare's Richard II: *A Retelling in Prose*
William Shakespeare's Richard III: *A Retelling in Prose*
William Shakespeare's Romeo and Juliet: *A Retelling in Prose*
William Shakespeare's The Taming of the Shrew: *A Retelling in Prose*
William Shakespeare's The Tempest: *A Retelling in Prose*
William Shakespeare's Timon of Athens: *A Retelling in Prose*
William Shakespeare's Titus Andronicus: *A Retelling in Prose*
William Shakespeare's Troilus and Cressida: *A Retelling in Prose*
William Shakespeare's Twelfth Night: *A Retelling in Prose*
William Shakespeare's The Two Gentlemen of Verona: *A Retelling in Prose*
William Shakespeare's The Two Noble Kinsmen: *A Retelling in Prose*
William Shakespeare's The Winter's Tale: *A Retelling in Prose*